MY NAME IS DELILAH

A Medical Love Story

Copyright©2005 by Verne E. Gilbert, M.D.

Front cover photograph: Sir William Osler, M.D., Chief of Medicine, examines a patient at the Johns Hopkins Hospital, circa 1904. The Alan Mason Chesney Medical Archives of the Johns Hopkins Medical Institution provided this photograph.

Front cover design by Verne E. Gilbert, M.D.

Published February 2006 by Smoky Mountain Press
P.O. Box 6855
Oak Ridge, TN 37831

ISBN: 0-9729795-1-4

MY NAME IS DELILAH

A Medical Love Story

Verne E. Gilbert, M.D.

Smoky Mountain Press

Oak Ridge

AUTHOR'S NOTE

This novel includes a nonfiction narrative—*The Romance of Bedside Diagnosis.* Patients' right to privacy and the admonition for secrecy in the Hippocratic oath preclude full disclosure of cases. Therefore, I have masked and altered clinical descriptions in this work except for the one in chapter eight (Never Examine Your Secretary) where permission for release of information has been granted.

Verne E. Gilbert, M.D.

How do I love thee? Let me
     count the ways.
I love thee to the depth and breadth
     and height
My soul can reach, when feeling
     out of sight
For the ends of Being and Ideal Grace.

Elisabeth Barrett Browning

CONTENTS

Chapter One

THE FOG

Early spring mornings are special in Western Pennsylvania—a sharp chill fills the air; the rising sun scatters reddish orange light on the frost like millions of sparkling sequins; and on blossoming pear trees, tiny buds become bright red cherries. And sometimes, Pittsburgh's rivers spread a creeping fog that engulfs the land, and as one moves through the gloom, the soul becomes overwhelmed by mystery and awe.

Delilah, dressed in a crisp new nursing uniform, slipped out into a billowing mist, pulled the collar of her coat tightly underneath her thin face then slowly walked to a van.

Eyes focused, arms tense, she carefully steered into heavy traffic. "Don't crash in this awful fog," she thought. "This road should take me to Heavenly Manor, that old nursing home on amber Street."

On the opposite side of the avenue, crawling with agonizing slowness, a procession of headlights wobbled toward her like twin yellow lanterns in an oriental parade. "I hope those cars won't swerve into my lane," she thought.

"Yes, I'm finished as a charge nurse for the hospital's intensive care unit. Ten years of continuous stress is enough. I've suffered too much as patients died; and I can't stand the tears. Delilah, what has your life wrought? You've saved lives? Yes. You've worn out your body? Yes. You've found a husband? No. Work. Sleep. Work. Sleep. That has been the pattern of your life. Enough is enough. You must stop. Now is the time to stop and reflect."

"Delilah, come quickly. Bed nine has arrested. Get the crash cart. Grab the shock paddles. Delilah, bed eight has stopped breathing. Quick, grab the ventilator mask. Delilah, bed seven has a high fever. Call the doctor. Delilah, bed three has dropped her blood pressure. It's zero. Quick, put in a line."

"Stop it. Stop it," she told herself. "Just finish this brief assignment in the nursing home then rest, exercise and prepare for your travels. Eventually, you'll find a new life. You can't save patients anymore. You can't save anyone anymore. Now, you must try to save yourself."

Chapter Two

THE ABYSS

Up for hours, Doctor Jerome Stern, a patient in Heavenly Manor's unit for Alzheimer's disease, sat beside the window waiting for dawn. But on this day, like so many recent days, morning sunlight barely penetrated the glass as dense fog engulfed the building.

"Those damn vapors have cheated me out of sunrise," he said to himself. "While dying in a nursing home, I can't even experience a small pleasure. Yes, my brain is shot—totally shot. I can't remember spoken words or simple tasks. Now, I'm stumbling while walking down the hall. But during my final days, I'll think about my practice and all my wonderful patients. I had great cases—spectacular diagnostic triumphs. I remember the teenage boy who suffered with high fever. I diagnosed acute brucellosis just by asking one question and palpating his large tender spleen. Yes, a great case—only one hour between hospitalization and confirmed diagnosis. And that young female hiker, misdiagnosed as a case of gas gangrene, I saved her leg by saying, 'you are the most beautiful girl in the face of this earth.' She wept, trusted my judgement and allowed the debridement of her wound.

Clearly, I remember that professor of English with fatal acute hepatitis. I saved his life by treating the hepatic coma with experimental exchange transfusions of blood.. 'Doctor Stern,' he said, 'you are a prince of medicine.'

But now, at age 54, I'm in this awful place just watching my mind slowly drift away. Today, I won't touch breakfast. The end can't come soon enough."

A male attendant opened the door to room 14 and delivered a tray of food. "Jerry, you're still losing weight. Doctor Thompson will force a feeding tube down your throat if you don't start eating."

Jerry slowly turned his face toward the window hoping to see a few beams of morning sunlight.

Chapter Three

THE ASSIGNMENT

High on a hill, Heavenly Manor rose out of the gloom like an old mysterious house seen in a horror movie—gray, dark and foreboding. Nervous about her assignment, Delilah found space in a parking lot then entered the building searching for the office of the director, Doctor John Thompson. Shortly, she found the right door, entered and noticed an elderly secretary sitting at a desk shuffling papers.

"I'm the temporary nurse chosen for the unit holding patients with Alzheimer's disease. I'm working for two weeks."

The secretary gave Delilah a scowl then pointed a finger over her shoulder. "Doctor Thompson will see you in that room."

A tall man with a white mustache stood up and extended his hand to Delilah. "You're quite young to work in a nursing home. Yes?"

"The agency offered me a cash bonus to take the position. I've been working for years in the intensive care unit at the University hospital. I'm burned out. I can't save patients anymore."

"My dear, there is no one to save at Heavenly Manor. All you need to do is dispense medications and make notes in charts. All patients are under control. Please, go to the third floor. The nurse on duty will give you instructions."

Delilah turned, entered the hallway then began climbing a spiral staircase as if advancing toward her doom. At the landing, she found a locked door, rang a bell, entered then spoke to a frail old nurse sitting at a desk. "I've been assigned to this unit for two weeks."

"Honey, you're a little young to work in a place like this."

"I'm burned out from years of hard work in intensive care. Too much stress and too many deaths. I can't save patients anymore."

"Don't worry, there's no one to save on this floor. Just push this cart down the hall, offer medications and make notes in charts if you see anything unusual. By the way, we have a tragic case in room 14. He's a physician and only 54 years old. He's suffering from rapidly advancing presenile dementia like that actress Rita Hayworth. He's not eating—you might need to feed him."

"What type of doctor was he?"

"An internist—a super diagnostician."

Promptly, Delilah placed her coat on a rack, grabbed the cart and began moving down the hall distributing medicines. Occasionally, she made a note in a chart, and eventually, reached room 14. Finding the door slightly ajar, she tapped on it with her knuckles then entered the room.

"I'm Delilah, the nurse on the floor."

"Where's the fat one?"

"She's retired. I'm working here for two weeks."

"Only two weeks."

"Yes. Have you eaten breakfast?

"I'm not hungry."

"Here, let me help you," Delilah said while filling a spoon with oatmeal.

She slowly lifted the food to his mouth then cleaned his chin with a napkin. "Please, take your fork and eat the omelet, it looks good."

"What's our name? You're beautiful."

"Delilah. My name is Delilah."

"You're so beautiful."

"Here, take these medications."

"What are they?"

"This is Zoloft—it's for depression."

"Take it away. It's making me sick."

"Here, take your Ativan."

"No, it's making me groggy."

"These drugs will keep you calm."

"I'm not depressed. My brain is shot."

"Please, you must cooperate."

"What's the use. My memory is gone."

"Please eat your eggs."

"You're so beautiful. What's your name?"

"My name is Delilah."

"May I touch your face—it's so lovely."

"Well. Well. I don't know."

"Please. You're so beautiful."

"OK. It's OK."

Slowly, with hesitation, Doctor Stern lifted a hand toward Delilah's face, and with two fingers, touched her high cheek bone, caressed it, then traced its course to her nose before brushing her lips.

Trembling, Delilah closed her eyes for a second or two. "You don't act like a demented patient."

Turning quickly, she moved to the door. "I'll send the aide to help you walk in the hall."

Delilah reached the desk in the hall and grabbed the arm of the chief nurse.

"Doctor Stern in bed 14 doesn't seem demented. He made a pass at me."

"Patients might do that before they die. Did he take his medications?"

"No, he said the drugs made him sick and groggy."

"You watch, the director will force a feeding tube down his throat."

"I would like to speak with Doctor Thompson about Doctor Stern. May I leave for a few minutes?"

"Sure, but he won't change any treatment."

Delilah turned, descended the long staircase and found the director sitting in his office.

"I'm sorry to bother you, but Doctor Stern, in bed 14, doesn't seem demented. His memory is gone but he doesn't talk like a man suffering with Alzheimer's disease."

"The court ordered him here after he stopped caring for himself. He is a case of presenile dementia. It started last year when he hospitalized patients then forgot about them. The medical center cancelled his staff privileges, the medical board removed his license and his wife divorced him."

"He refused all medications this morning. I would like to stop the sedatives and tranquilizing drugs to see how he behaves."

Doctor Thompson frowned and walked behind his desk. "Delilah, this is your first day at Heavenly Manor. Patients in this facility can be upsetting, indeed. Doctor Stern's case is sad but he can't even walk without stumbling. He'll be dead within the year. I've seen it before. Please, don't break your heart."

"What harm can come to the patient if all drugs are stopped for a few days?"

"We keep all patients under tight control at Heavenly Manor. But since you feel strongly about this case, I'll order the chief nurse to halt his medications for three days. Delilah, I hope you will like Heavenly manor. It is not stressful. Please, I would like you to consider working as a full-time nurse."

"Thank you, but I've taken this position for two weeks—that's all."

Later that afternoon, Delilah peeled off her white uniform then began dressing in a cycling outfit. Carefully, she stepped into bike pants, tights, and then, added a warm jersey. Finally, she slipped on a windbreaker colored screaming yellow. Next, she inflated the tires of her Trek 5200 road bike to a hard 150 pounds then pushed it onto the road in front of her house. "This sport provides wonderful release of stress. This terrific machine accelerates with even the slightest stroke of the pedals. I love it. I love it."

Turning onto a small path, she began a long steady climb. "I can't wait to spend more time on this lovely bike. My cycling trip in Europe is only six weeks away. And in 13 days, I'm leaving the nursing profession for a long time. I need rest—desperately need rest. And then? What will you do with your life? I don't know and I don't care. For now, I must try to save my soul."

The road became steeper and Delilah began breathing hard, but quickly, she flipped a lever and the bike shifted into a lower gear before reaching the summit of a huge hill. After stopping and gazing at the lovely green valley below, she grabbed the drops of her handle bars, clicked shoes into pedals, cocked her head upward and pointed the bike downhill.

Faster and faster, power in her legs, power through the curves, she accelerated in a screaming descent with her long auburn hair billowing in the wind beneath her helmet. "I wonder if Doctor Stern will look better in the morning?" she thought.

The next day, Delilah stepped out of her house with a bounce in her step but didn't understand her cheerful mood. "This fog is like pea soup—worse then yesterday."

She carefully steered her car on the long road to Heavenly manor, and then, on arrival, climbed the long staircase to see patients with Alzheimer's disease.

"Guess what?" the chief nurse said as she entered the unit. "The aide says that Doctor Stern is eating breakfast while sitting in a chair."

"That's interesting. I can't wait to see him."

Methodically, Delilah moved the cart down the hall dispensing medications and made a few notes in charts. "I can see why families need a nursing home for patients with Alzheimer's disease," she thought. Eventually, she reached room 14.

"You look alive," Delilah said on entering the room.

"What's your name? You're beautiful."

"My name is Delilah. I'm here for another 13 days."

"My brain is dead. I can't remember spoken words."

"How long have you been ill?"

"I'm not sure."

"You don't behave like a victim of Alzheimer's disease."

"You're so beautiful."

"Please, Doctor Stern. I'm trying to help you."

"I need to get out of here."

"Where will you go? Who will care for you?"

"I don't know."

"Do you remember if you had a brain scan before entering Heavenly Manor?"

"I don't know."

"Please, stick out your arm. I need to measure your blood pressure."

Delilah carefully wrapped the blood pressure cuff around the arm. "It's 120/80. Excellent."

"You're so lovely. May I touch your face again."

"Well, I'm not sure."

"Please. Please."

"OK. It's OK."

Doctor Stern slowly lifted a shaking hand toward Delilah's face

10

then caressed her cheek, chin and inside of her neck.

"You need to see a neurologist. I have a friend who will give you an excellent examination. Are you willing to go?

"Sure, but my brain is dead. It's hopeless."

Quickly, Delilah left the room descended the long staircase to the ground floor of Heavenly Manor and found Doctor Thompson.

"I'm sorry to bother you again about Doctor Stern. I believe he needs an examination by a neurologist. I have a friend who is an expert."

"Delilah, I agree that he is more alert but the diagnosis seems correct. I have no objection if you wish to find another opinion. Since the court made him a ward of Heavenly Manor, I must sanction all major actions. I hope you will consider working here. We desperately need nurses."

Chapter Four

THE RISING

Morning greeted Delilah with cold crisp air as she placed Doctor Stern in her car for a ride to the physician's office building. In every direction, she noticed small green leaves on branches, red blossoms bursting from azalea plants and birds dashing about, chirping loudly. "Spring has arrived with gusto," she thought. "I hope Doctor Stern will have a new beginning too."

"I'm weak," Jerry Stern declared. "I'll need a wheel chair."

"You must eat. You look like a man just rescued from a concentration camp."

Doctor Terrance Smith greeted Delilah warmly in his office. "It's nice to see you again."

"This is Doctor Jerome Stern. He has lost his memory."

"How long have you been ill?"

"Awhile."

Delilah quickly interjected. "It started last year when he hospitalized patients then forgot about them."

"What type of medicine have you practiced?"

"Internal medicine and infectious diseases."

"You specialized in both fields at the same time?"

"Yes. I had great cases."

"That doesn't sound like a patient with Alzheimer's disease. How did you get into a nursing home?"

"The court ordered him there when he stopped caring for himself," Delilah added.

"Do you have a wife?"

"Gone. She divorced me."

"I see. And Delilah, you don't believe he has Alzheimer's disease?"

"He talks normally but was sedated and tranquilized at Heavenly Manor. Also, he made a pass at me."

"Really! Really! That's interesting."

"She's so beautiful," Doctor Stern said in a low voice.

"I agree. But how long have you had trouble walking?"

"I don't know."

"What day is it?"

"I don't know."

"Who is president of the United States?"

Doctor Stern just shrugged and looked plaintively at Delilah.

"Please say for me the following statement: Around the rugged rock the rapid rabbit ran."

"Around—around."

"Delilah, you wait here. I'll examine him in the next room."

Forty-five minutes later, Doctor Smith returned with his patient in tow. "He certainly has lost memory and he has a weird gait too."

"Doctor Stern, I would like to place you in the hospital for tests including a MRI scan of the brain. Many diseases mimic Alzheimer's disease such as, to name a few, brain tumors, vitamin deficiencies, hormonal imbalances, multiple sclerosis, strokes, lupus, infections and hydrocephalus. Hydrocephalus is the enlargement of the fluid-filled chambers in the brain—the ventricles. If this occurs, brain tissue is compressed and the result may be a temporary loss of memory."

"You will need Doctor Thompson's permission to hospitalize Doctor Stern," Delilah said. "He is the guardian for the court."

"I'll call him. I'm sure it's just a formality. May I proceed, Doctor Stern?"

"Sure, but it's hopeless. My brain is shot."

Doctor Smith buzzed his nurse who came with a wheelchair.

The neurologist squeezed Doctor Stern's shoulder. "I'll see you tonight after reviewing your tests."

"When shall I return?" Delilah asked.

"Be in his room by eight p.m."

Turning to Doctor Stern, he said, "You've been most fortunate to have Delilah interested in your case."

"She is so beautiful."

Delilah blushed as a nurse placed the patient in a wheelchair for the ride to the adjacent hospital.

Later that evening, Delilah sat beside Jerry's bed anxiously waiting for the neurologist. Soon, he arrived sporting a huge smile.

"I have interesting news," he said.

"First, I found low blood levels of vitamin B12 and folic acid. Your brain can't function without these critical B vitamins. I hope it works better after I correct these abnormalities. I'll give you pills and shots, starting tonight. More importantly, however, the MRI scan of the brain has revealed an enlargement of your ventricles. The cells in these spaces might not be absorbing fluid at a normal rate which would cause expansion of the chamber—a condition called normal pressure hydrocephalus. Have you experienced an auto accident or trauma to your head?"

"I had a concussion after my car slid off the road in an ice storm."

"Blood in your ventricles might have damaged tissues that absorbs fluid and this might have caused hydrocephalus," Doctor Smith stated. "Now, I'm going to perform a spinal tap to analyze the fluid for signs of infection. Also, I intend to draw off a large volume of liquid to relieve the pressure in your brain. If your memory and walking improves in a few days, you might benefit from the placement of a shunt in your ventricle to drain fluid into the abdomen. This procedure should correct the hydrocephalus and might cure your "Alzheimer's disease.""

A nurse entered the room with a large tray for the spinal tap procedure, and promptly, Doctor Smith placed Doctor Stern on his side, cleansed his lower back with iodine, numbed a small area with novocaine, then inserted a long needle into the spinal canal. Instantly, fluid began dripping into vials.

"Now, I'm draining spinal fluid to decompress the ventricles in your brain. How do you feel? Can you tell any difference?"

"Better. Better. My headache is gone. My mind feels clear."

"Good. In several days, if you're thinking better and walking smoother, I'll ask a neurosurgeon to insert a shunt into your ventricle. Indeed, you might have a normal pressure hydrocephalus. The name, however, is a misnomer since the pressure really rises intermittently during the day. Tomorrow, I'll return in the afternoon."

"I'm leaving too," Delilah declared. "I have 12 more days of work in Heavenly Manor."

The next evening, Delilah found Doctor Stern sitting in a chair reading a magazine. He stood up and announced, "I'm feeling better. My headache is gone. Look, I can walk smoothly again. There's hope for my brain and there's hope for my life."

"Has Doctor Smith returned?"

"Yes! Yes! He sent a neurosurgeon to examine me, a Doctor McGinness. In the morning, he'll insert a plastic tube into the ventricle of my brain to drain the fluid into my abdominal cavity. I remember your name— it's Delilah and you're beautiful—really beautiful."

Tears welled up into Delilah's eyes and then she began sobbing, an uncontrollable sobbing. "What's your name?" she asked.

"Jerry. My name is Jerry."

"May I touch your face?"

"Sure. Sure."

Deliberately, unhurried, Delilah raised a shaking hand toward Jerry and caressed his cheeks, eyelids, nose and lips. "Jerry, you are beautiful."

Early the next morning, Delilah showered then dashed to her car in the darkness trying to reach the hospital before the staff from the operating room snatched Jerry away for brain surgery. "Damn it. This nasty fog has returned."

For awhile, the car creeped slowly down the road, Delilah became agitated, but soon, the route cleared and the car sped forward allowing her to reach the hospital before sunrise. She arrived at room 115 then tapped lightly on the door. "It's your nurse from Heavenly Manor. May I come in?"

Delilah opened the door, slipped silently into the room, and found Jerry sitting bolt upright in bed, ghost like, illuminated by a faint yellow light.

"What's your name?" Delilah said.

"Jerry. My name is Jerry."

"May I kiss your face, Jerry?"

"Sure. Sure."

Suddenly, Jerry lunged forward, grabbed Delilah and pressed himself against her body, stroking her hair. "I need to see your face each morning. I need to see your face at supper. I need to hold you all night long." Tears streamed down from his eyes.

Delilah wiped the moisture from his face. "Jerry, I'm leaving for Europe in six weeks."

"I'll go too," he blurted out.

"Jerry," she whispered, "it is complicated. We'll talk after your surgery. For now, just let me hold you."

The door opened and a tall nurse entered with a long cart. "You'll need to release him, Mrs. Stern. The operating room is waiting."

"I'm just his nurse from Heavenly Manor."

Promptly, Jerry placed his body on the moving bed then quickly disappeared down the hallway.

"Wait in the surgical lounge," an aide instructed Delilah. "A doctor will speak with you after the patient is placed in the recovery room."

For Delilah, two hours passed like a lifetime, but finally, a tall figure, clad in green entered the waiting area. "Doctor Stern's family, please."

"How is he doing," Delilah inquired. "I'm his nurse from Heavenly Manor."

"The surgery went well. The ventricular fluid is now draining into his abdominal cavity through a small plastic tube. I am confident his surgery will relieve the hydrocephalus. I can't predict, however, if he will regain memory."

"He improved after the spinal tap."

"That's a good sign," the surgeon said as he extended his hand before leaving the room.

"Thank you, doctor," Delilah said. Quickly, she rose from the chair, left the lounge and departed for the nursing home.

Several hours later, in the recovery room, Doctor Terrance Smith approached Jerry after he became fully awake.

"Jerry, I have high hopes that your memory will return."

"I can't go back to the nursing home," he stammered almost crying. "They will kill me."

The doctor held Jerry's hand. "You have a complicated legal situation that requires expert advice. The hospital's attorney is mister Leon Rittenbaum, a legal super star. He might petition the court to release you. I'll call him."

Jerry began sobbing—an uncontrollable sobbing. "Thank you. Thank you. I can't go back. I can't go back."

Chapter Five

THE ATTORNEY

Later that evening, Delilah found her favorite patient sitting in bed with a large bandage around his head. Jerry smiled. "The surgeon did a great job. He drilled a small hole in my skull then placed a drain in the ventricle of my brain. It doesn't hurt. But please, tell me why you are leaving for Europe?"

"Tomorrow. Let's talk tomorrow when you're stronger."

Someone began knocking on Jerry's door.

"Come in," Delilah yelled.

A tall man with white hair strode briskly into the room. He wore a dark blue suit with pinstripes and a small white handkerchief dangled informally out of his breast pocket. He extended his hand.

"I'm Leon Rittenbaum, III," he announced. "Please call me Leon. Doctor Smith spoke with me about your difficult situation and its my great pleasure to assist you. You are a walking, breathing, living miracle. No person has ever recovered from Alzheimer's disease. You did it. I'm dumbstruck and awed by your story."

"How will I pay you?" Jerry questioned. "I don't have income. I don't have assets."

"Let's not worry about that right now. If necessary, I'll do the work pro bono."

"You know that the court ordered me into the nursing home?"

"Yes."

"I can't go back. They might put a feeding tube down my throat."

"Calm down. I'll check the records, find who petitioned the court to place you in Heavenly Manor and learn which attorney worked your case. He'll talk to me and give valuable information. What happened to your home, bank accounts and other assets?"

"I don't know."

"Your wife cleaned you out?"

"Probably."

"Who has been paying your expenses at the nursing home?"

"I don't know."

"Don't worry. I'll get the answer when I meet with the director of Heavenly Manor. He might have received a lump sum of money to care for you or your wife might be sending monthly checks. It is one or the other. In the morning, I'll visit the nursing home while my staff checks your court records. Please, sign this form. It gives me your power of attorney for 30 days. With this document, I'll be able to negotiate, set up a bank account and secure a visa card for you. I'll need an address."

"He can stay with me at 730 Midway Lane," Delilah offered. "He'll need good nursing care."

"OK," Leon answered with a grin. "Please, sign this sheet on the dotted line. I'll block your return to Heavenly Manor with a court injunction."

Jerry pumped Leon's hand. "Thanks," Jerry said. "You are a ray of hope."

Leon patted him on the shoulder. "Don't worry. I intend to take care of you."

The next day, during his morning coffee break, the director of Heavenly Manor received a buzz from his secretary.

"There is a distinguished attorney here to see you regarding Doctor Stern. He says that he needs an urgent meeting."

Leon entered the office and extended his hand and card to Doctor Thompson.

"I am Leon Rittenbaum, III. I represent Jerome Stern who has given me his power of attorney to negotiate. At the moment, he is in the hospital recovering from brain surgery. A neurosurgeon has placed a shunt into the ventricle of his brain to relieve hydrocephalus, which has caused his loss of memory. He is rapidly improving. Apparently, you and others have wrongly labeled him as a case of Alzheimer's disease. Who has been paying his expenses at Heavenly Manor?"

"We receive Doctor Stern's social security check each month."

"How much?"

"About $3000."

"In the future, please send these checks to my office."

"I'm not sure I can do that."

"I think you can and I hope you will," Leon stated in a threatening tone. "Do you own Heavenly Manor or do you just work here?"

"I'm a part owner but there are other investors."

"I see. Please, I wish to make myself perfectly clear. You and others at Heavenly Manor have wrongfully diagnosed Doctor Stern and nearly caused his death from hydrocephalus. You have inflicted on him terrible pain and suffering. In the morning, I intend to file a lawsuit against you and your investors for the amount of five million dollars if my conditions are not met by five p.m. today."

"What conditions?"

"First, you must return to Jerome Stern all social security checks you have cashed. Second, you must send him a check in the amount of $50,000 to compensate him for the suffering he received at Heavenly manor. Here is the agreement. You and your partners must sign this document and present the funds to my office by five p.m. This will be your only opportunity to settle this lawsuit."

"I'll speak with my investors, immediately," Doctor Thompson stammered in a low voice.

Leon extended his hand to the director then turned and left the office with quick long strides.

After reaching his car, Leon called his office using his cell phone. His secretary came on the line.

"Sharon," he said, "put Johnston on the line."

"Johnston here, sir."

"What have you learned about that old court action against Jerome Stern?"

"Stanley Jones represented Mrs. Stern on all court matters."

"OK, give Sharon his telephone number. I'll call him in a few minutes. Also, please file a temporary injunction with the court to block Doctor Stern's return to Heavenly Manor. Please, have it in place by this afternoon."

"Considered it done, sir."

"Also, Johnston, I want you and Avery to complete a brief for a five million dollar lawsuit against Heavenly Manor and all its investors. Find the list of owners from the tax roles and get the dates of the consultations by Doctors Terrance Smith and William McGuinness from their offices. Doctor Stern's diagnosis is normal pressure hydrocephalus not Alzheimer's disease. Look up this condition on the Internet. You will see that is a curable cause of lost memory. I'll need it by nine a.m. if Heavenly Manor refuses to settle."

"Consider it done, sir."

"Also, Johnston, please work with the social security department and have Doctor Stern's checks sent to his savings account which I will ask the bank to set up. They will send the account number of our office today."

"Consider it done, sir."

"Thank you, Johnson. Please put Sharon back on the line."

Leon's secretary promptly came back on the telephone.

"Sharon," Leon said, "please call the president of Pittsburgh National Bank and patch him in to me when he answers.

21

Soon, Leon heard a familiar voice and said, "Hi John. This is Leon. I need a little favor this morning. I have a client in the hospital who needs an immediate savings account and a visa card. His name is Doctor Jerome Stern, 730 Midway Lane, Pittsburgh. Please forward the account number and visa card to my office this afternoon. I have his power of attorney."

"Sure, Leon. It's good to hear from you. I'll see you at the club."

"Sharon, are you still on the line?"

"Yes."

"Please, call attorney Stanley Jones and patch him in to me."

Soon, Leon heard the voice of attorney Jones.

"Good morning Stanley, this is Leon. How are you?"

"Fine, Leon, what can I do for you?"

"Do you remember the court case against Doctor Jerome Stern—the man had Alzheimer's disease. Do you still represent his wife?"

"No," she left town and the state too, I believe."

"What happened to the man's home, bank accounts and other assets?"

"I'm not at liberty to say—you know that."

"Do you have Mrs. Stern's address?"

"No."

"I guess you won't release any more information—will you?"

"No."

"OK, Stanley, I'm grateful for this conversation. Have a nice day."

Later that evening, Leon returned to the hospital and found Delilah sitting beside Jerry's bed.

"Jerry, how are you feeling?" he asked.

"Much better. I'm walking smoother and my brain is retaining

22

more words and events."

"I have news. First, it appears that your wife left the state after cleaning you out. I think it will be hard to track her down and sue. Second, I met Doctor Thompson at Heavenly Manor and he generously agreed to return your social security checks. Apparently, someone had you declared disabled and placed you on social security. Also, Doctor Thompson sent to my office a check in your name in the amount of $50,000 to compensate you for suffering you might have experienced at Heavenly Manor. I have deposited those funds in your new savings account at Pittsburgh National bank. Here is your account number. Furthermore, they have issued you a visa card. Here it is. By the way, all future social security checks will be deposited electronically into your account and my staff has filed an injunction to block your return to Heavenly Manor. The hearing will take place in four weeks.

"Wow! Wow!" Jerry shouted as he grabbed both of Leon's hands. "You really are a legal super star."

"It is my pleasure to serve you. You have risen from the abyss with the help of Delilah and expert doctors. Is there anything else I can do?"

"Yes, call the chairman of the state's medical board and explain to him my situation. I want my medical license returned as soon as possible."

"I'll do that in the morning. Is there anything else?"

"One small item," Jerry stated in a weak voice. "I need one of those hand held dictation machines to write about my great cases."

"Medical articles?" Delilah asked.

"No, I'm going to write a book about the magic of bedside diagnosis. I want to turn back the medical clock to the end of the nineteenth century when physicians diagnosed illnesses without laboratory tests. I've had many great cases, patients with pathos— real pathos."

"Do you have a title?"

"Yes—*The Romance of Bedside Diagnosis*. I've been working on this book for years. My wife discarded my manuscript but its typed in my mind ready for printing."

"That sounds wonderful. Call Sharon, my secretary. She'll get the machine for you and one of my girls from the typing pool might work for you at night."

"That's great," Jerry said effusively while shaking Leon's hand again.

"Jerry, I need to go. Stay well. I'll speak with the medical board as soon as possible."

"I'm going too," Delilah announced. "I must be at the nursing home early in the morning."

Delilah gently kissed Jerry on the cheek then left the room.

The next day, just after lunch, Jerry called the medical center. "Give me the chief of staff."

Soon, Jerry heard the voice of Doctor Thomas Osborne.

"Tom, this is Jerry Stern."

"Jerry, how are you. I heard that you are at Heavenly Manor. How are you doing with your Alzheimer's disease?"

"I've recovered. I never had Alzheimer's disease."

"That's ridiculous. No one regains their memory."

"Tom. I have been suffering with normal pressure hydrocephalus and I'm in the hospital recovering from brain surgery. I had a shunt placed in my ventricle to relieve the pressure. My memory has returned. I want my staff privileges back and I'm opening a new office."

"Over my dead body!"

"What!"

"Jerry, I said you will get your staff privileges back only over my dead body. After you forgot about those patients you hospitalized on the ninth floor, I stepped in and cared for them. Remember?"

"No, I don't remember."

"See what I mean," Doctor Osborne shouted over the line. "You are a menace to patients and the hospital will not take you back."

Jerry just stared at the telephone. Doctor Osborne had hung up. Several minutes later, Leon called.

"Jerry, I have bad news for you. I spoke with the chairman of the medical board and he refused to consider returning your medical license. He said that you placed patient's lives in jeopardy and you might do it again if your shunt gets clogged. He'll block any attempt you make to practice medicine in this state."

"That's terrible," Jerry murmured over the line. "I just spoke with the chief of staff at the medical center and he said the same thing. He sounded angry."

"That call was a mistake, Jerry. You need to concentrate on regaining your health and take time to smell the roses. Be glad that your brain is working again. Be happy that you still are alive!"

"Leon," Jerry said in a quiet voice, "I'm only 54 years old. What shall I do with the rest of my life?"

"Jerry, calm down. You have an interesting idea for a book— work on it. Eventually, you will find the direction for life. Trust me. Everything will work out. But don't take any small job that will jeopardize your checks from social security. You'll need those funds."

"Thanks, Leon. You've been very kind. You are a great lawyer."

Crestfallen, head down, Jerry moved to an open window and gazed out at a blue sky filled with columns of white clouds. A cool wind caressed his face, his nerves calmed and he began musing about the shattering events of the past few days. "A beautiful angel of mercy snatched me from the abyss. I had been rapidly sinking into blackness in the nursing home. Delilah! That's her name. Did she appear as a reincarnation of Sampson's Delilah? I'm not sure. She said, 'My Name is Delilah,' and my soul soared to the heavens—in rapture; and at the sight of her beauty, my body tingled. No wonder Sampson divulged his secret when Delilah asked, 'Wherein thy great strength lieth?'

Sampson was a Nazarite—a man dedicated to god. And wherein does my great strength lieth? Of course, it has been in my long devotion to the ancient art of medicine.

Since leaving academic life, 20 years have vanished in a blink of an eye, and sadly, I've watched high technology dull physician's skills, the gifts of sages. Yes, the voices of Rene Laennec, William Osler and others have been stilled but not silenced. In almost a religious pilgrimage, I've followed their cherished footsteps and witnessed the value of their wisdom. I must write about this craft, an art that endures and surges like a rolling tide, caressing the lives of patients."

Suddenly, Jerry pulled away from the window, and with emotion rising and tears flowing, he began scribbling notes on a pad while recalling great cases and the romance of bedside diagnosis.

Chapter Six

THE ATHLETE

Several hours later, a tall woman, dressed in a dark business suit, entered the room with a package under her arm. "I'm Melinda, from Mr. Rittenbaum's office. I've brought you a dictating machine. As you finish each chapter of your book, deliver the cassette to us and I'll type the work at night. I charge $9 an hour."

"That's very kind of you, Melinda. Your price is fair. I can pay for the services."

"When will you start?"

"Probably tonight. This book has been rolling around in my brain for several years."

Melinda smiled and turned to leave the room. "I'll wait to hear from you."

A nurse entered with a wheelchair. "I'm taking you for another MRI scan of your brain. Doctor McGinness needs to see if your ventricles are shrinking.'

"I'm sure they are smaller. My memory is almost back to normal."

Before long, Jerry returned to his room and found Delilah sitting in a chair dressed in a bright red warm-up suit.

"I'm surprised to see you here."

"I've been fired. Doctor Thompson thinks I'm a troublemaker but he paid me for two weeks work plus the bonus promised by the employment agency."

"Why the jumpsuit?"

"I'm training for my cycling trip in Europe. It starts in the middle of May."

"Cycling in Europe? Where? Why?"

"Look, Jerry," Delilah said in a low voice, "I'm burned out from years of working in the ICU. I can't stand the stress. I can't stand the deaths and the tears. I need rest and plan to force the beauty of nature into my soul. I've been planning this trip for a long time."

"Where will you go?"

"First, I plan to cycle from Prague to Vienna. Much of the route is along the beautiful Danube river."

"That's incredible! Totally incredible!"

"Next, I'll fly to Marseilles, rent a van then drive to the gorgeous Luberon valley. This area, with old perched villages, is where Peter Mayle lived when he wrote *A Year in Provence*. I want to enjoy scenery and the wonderful French food and wine."

"Oh, my God. That sounds too good to be true."

"Then, I'll cross the Rhone river, cycle among the vineyards and visit the old Roman city of Nimes and the Pont du Gard."

"That's unbelievable. And then?"

"Next, I'll fly to Florence, suck beauty and art into my soul then pedal into the spectacular green hills of Tuscanny. This will be the most difficult part of the journey because of long steep roads."

Tears filled Jerry's eyes and he hung his head. "And what about me? I can't live one day without you. I see your lovely face in my mind all the time, especially at night. When you come in the room, I tremble. When you leave, my heart sinks. I need to hold you at night, every night. I love you! I love you!"

Delilah moved forward, placed her arms around Jerry's neck and began whispering in his ear.

"Jerry dear, don't worry. I'm taking you with me. We'll cycle together all day, eat long meals in romantic restaurants and make love every night. I won't let you go. I'm going to make you an athlete—the nursing home's athlete."

"I don't own a bicycle."

"You can buy a great bike after you've been discharged from the hospital. For now, you must eat as much as you can to gain weight. Also, you must push yourself as hard as possible in physical therapy to build up your muscles. I'm not taking a weak man on this long journey. We'll pound the beauty of Europe into our souls and freeze time. We'll put this nasty world on hold. Jerry, it will be you and me against the wind. It will be you and me—one with our bikes. It will be you and me experiencing delicious exhaustion. Just you and me, Jerry, eating wonderful food, tasting delicious wines and sucking in incredible scenery. It will be just you and me, Jerry—together."

Delilah pressed herself against Jerry's body as someone knocked on the door then pushed it open. "I'm an aide from physical therapy. I'm picking up Doctor Jerome Stern."

"Let's go," Delilah instructed. "I'll speak with the therapist and order your treatment."

Soon, the group reached a large room filled with exercise machines. Delilah looked around."Let me speak with the chief in charge of rehabilitation."

A tall muscular man approached and extended his hand.

"This is Doctor Jerome Stern," Delilah explained. "Recently, he's been dying in Heavenly Manor with Alzheimer's disease. But now, he is recovering after the placement of a shunt into his brain. I need you to develop this man—make him an athlete. He is cycling from Prague to Vienna in just six weeks."

"You're joking. This man is a bag of skin and bones."

Jerry grabbed Delilah's arm. "We're cycling together in Europe on a special holiday." He beamed.

"I'm his private trainer. I need you to build him up as fast as possible. You must push him—push him to exhaustion. Please, use cross training procedures and exercise him with treadmill, cycling, weight lifting and climbing machines. If he develops pain in his muscles—ice him down. Also, at the end of each day, he'll need a total body massage."

"That's ridiculous but I'll do it."

Delilah turned to leave. "Work hard, Jerry. I'll see you tomorrow night."

Later, Jerry returned from physical therapy in a state of total exhaustion and collapsed in bed. But just before falling asleep, a nurse entered the room, approached him then carefully removed the bandage from his head. "The wound and stitches look good."

Later in the evening, Doctor McGinness arrived and gently shook Jerry's shoulder until he stirred.

"I've reviewed the MRI scan of your brain and find that your ventricles are shrinking. You can go home in a few days if they continue to improve. Are you going back to the nursing home?"

"I'm staying with my nurse, Delilah."

"That's fine. We'll need one more scan before you go."

Promptly, Jerry slipped into a deep death-like sleep.

Chapter Seven

THE REPORTER

Early the next morning, the door to Jerry's room received a light knock, and suddenly, a smiling bearded face appeared in the opening of the door. "Hi," the small man said. "I'm John Davis from the Post-Gazette. I write articles on health and sciences. Doctor Stern, my sources in the hospital have informed me that you are recovering from Alzheimer's disease. This is exciting news. My newspaper is doing an important piece on this condition and the editor believes that your story will make a great contribution. We are thrilled to hear the news."

"My memory has returned but I never had Alzheimer's disease. Doctors gave me the wrong diagnosis."

"Really! Really!"

"Yes, but I don't see the point of this discussion. I want privacy. I'll suffer extreme embarrassment if you place my case in print since I've practiced in this community for years."

Mr. Davis presented Jerry his card. "Trust me, I'm a professional who will mask your identity. I wouldn't do anything to hurt you. Printing this report will provide a real service to others. Please, call my editor James Perkins. He'll vouch for my voracity and the integrity of the newspaper."

"Look," Jerry said after a long thoughtful pause. "I'm on social security and have been declared disabled. I have no other source of income and my illness has prevented me from working again. Will there be a stipend for this interview?"

"Sure," my editor is desperate to learn about your miraculous recovery. He believes the story might help many people with symptoms of Alzheimer's disease."

"I'll make you a deal. I'll give this interview if your newspaper buys me a bicycle."

"What type of bike?"

"A road bike—a Trek 5200. The Bike Zoo sells it. The shop is on Fifth Avenue."

Mr. Davis stood up to leave and extended his hand. "I'll discuss your proposal with my editor and call you back."

"I'll need a 54 centimeter frame," Jerry shouted as the man left.

Troubled, lost in thought about his long illness, Jerry went back to reviewing notes for his books. Several hours later, his telephone rang and the voice of John Davis appeared on the line. "We have a deal. I'm coming back this afternoon for the interview. What is a good time?"

"I'm exercising everyday in physical therapy. Let's talk after four o'clock."

Later, John Davis knocked on Jerry's door then entered the room pushing a purple bicycle. He smiled from ear to ear. "Here is your new Trek 5200. The frame is made of woven carbon fibers."

Jerry parked the bike against the wall. "It looks beautiful."

"Let's get started," Mr. Davis said while pulling on a long notebook. "Please, I need you to speak candidly and trust that I will mask your identity. I'll make you some other type of professional. OK?"

"That sounds good to me."

"Let's start at the beginning. When did you first notice that you were losing your memory?"

"It started last year. On entering a room at home, I forgot the purpose of being there. I found that irritating but not upsetting. But then, my wife became progressively disturbed when I began forgetting a variety of little tasks. Soon, I neglected to order tests needed for patients visiting my office. I felt exhausted, went on a small vacation, but rapidly became worse. A crisis developed after I hospitalized two patients but forgot to visit them."

"That's awful. They sat in the hospital with no one to care for them?"

Jerry put his head down and frowned. "Yes, indeed. The nurses on the ninth floor called the chief of staff who proceeded to treat these patients. He called me and arranged an emergency meeting with a committee of physicians who sanction credentials in the hospital. They withdrew my staff privileges. My wife had me evaluated by a psychiatrist who treated me for depression. Then, she filed for divorce and petitioned the court to transfer me to Heavenly Manor after I stopped eating and caring for myself. I lost weight, couldn't remember spoken words then had progressive difficulty with walking."

"How did you feel about all of this?"

"Despair. Blackness. I felt my body spinning into a dark hole. I could think but watched with anxiety as my mind decayed. No, I think a better word is rot. I remained in bed and watched my mind rot."

"How awful. What happened next?"

"The nurse on my floor retired and they brought in a temporary replacement, an angel of mercy who fed me cereal. I touched her lovely face.

"You made a pass at her?"

"I guess so. She looked beautiful."

"This is terrific. This is not only a tale concerning a miraculous recovery but it's also a love story—a beautiful love story."

"Maybe."

"Tell me more," John Davis pleaded.

"The nurse asked the director of Heavenly Manor to stop my medications since I was nauseated and groggy. They had been giving me tranquilizers and sedatives. I became more alert, and the next day, she brought me to Doctor Terrance Smith, a neurologist who hospitalized me for tests. They revealed a severe deficiency of vitamin B12 and folic acid. These chemicals are critical for the function of the brain. Also, the MRI scan of my brain revealed enlarged ventricles.

These spaces hold fluid, and the increased pressure, Doctor Smith said, compressed brain tissue causing the loss of memory. The condition is called normal pressure hydrocephalus. The name, however, is wrong since the pressure in the ventricles rises during the day. My memory began returning after Doctor smith tapped my spinal canal and removed a large volume of fluid to relieve pressure on my cerebral cortex. My walking also improved."

"You had problems walking?"

"Yes, but now it's perfect."

"Please continue."

"The next day, Doctor McGuinness, a neurosurgeon, placed a tube into the ventricle of my brain. It is called a shunt. He led the tube under the skin and into my abdominal cavity to permanently drain the fluid. Now, I feel fine. My memory has returned. I'm cured."

"Wow. That's great. But I don't understand why you didn't have these tests performed after you lost your memory?"

"I don't know. I was diagnosed as a case of presenile dementia—that's Alzheimer's disease in younger patients."

"This is a tremendous story. But why do you want the bicycle rather than cash?"

"I'm traveling to Europe on an exotic cycling journey. I have just six weeks to build up my muscles."

"Where are you going?"

"Delilah and I are biking from Prague to Vienna then into the Luberon Valley in France. Finally, we'll fly into Florence, enjoy the art then challenge the hills in Tuscanny."

"Wow, that's incredible. Who is Delilah?"

"She's the nurse who saved my brain. I plan to be with her the rest of my life."

"This is a love story—a medical love story."

"I guess so. There is nothing more to tell. I'm waiting for Doctor McGinness to order my discharge. Then, I'll start training on this beautiful bike."

"Are you going to practice medicine again?"

"No. The state's medical board of examiners have refused to return my license."

"I'm sorry to hear that," John Davis asserted. "It seems to me, the main message of this yarn is that patients with lost memory must receive expert medical evaluation. Again, I wish to assure you that our newspaper will mask your identity. The article will appear next Monday."

"It might be helpful if you speak with Doctor Terrance Smith," Jerry added. "He'll give you a long list of conditions that mimic Alzheimer's disease."

"I'll call him. That's a good tip."

"Now, I must rest. I'm exhausted from exercising in physical therapy."

John Davis extended his hand, turned then left the room.

Immediately, Jerry collapsed on the bed and fell into a long, deep sleep.

Chapter Eight

THE WAITING

Jerry awoke with a start and found Delilah sitting beside him on the bed. She planted a kiss on his cheek then began massaging his back and shoulders.

"Did you have a long ride today?" he asked while observing her bright red warm-up suit.

"I had a wonderful morning. I can't wait until you join me on my cycling routes. How did you get that gorgeous Trek 5200 bicycle in your room?"

"A reporter presented the bicycle as a gift from his newspaper after I consented to an interview regarding my recovery from Alzheimer's disease. Apparently, I've become a celebrity-patient in the hospital and the news leaked out. Please, take the bicycle to your house for safe keeping."

"This Trek needs a few modifications for our European adventures. First, the rear cluster should have a gear of 34 teeth so you can climb hills. Second, you'll need to install a larger seat and add a gel pad to prevent soreness in your buttocks. Last, you must replace the tires with the high performance Vredestein brand. They are made in Holland and have 50 percent less rolling resistance than other tires on the market."

"You're a real cycling expert. By the way, the nurse says Doctor McGuinness ordered my last MRI scan of the brain. I'm sure he'll order my discharge if he is satisfied."

Delilah grabbed the bicycle. "I"ll take the machine to the Bike Zoo and get it ready. We'll start training after you buy a complete cycling outfit."

In the morning, Jerry completed his final brain scan, and several hours later, the neurosurgeon entered the room, unsmiling. "There has been no additional shrinkage of your ventricles. Also, there is a little blood at the bottom of one of the chambers."

"What happened? I feel great."

"I'm not sure. It is possible that the tube might have irritated the walls of the ventricles. I'd like to observe you in the hospital for one more week."

"I'm feeling good. I'd like to leave the hospital."

"Doctor Stern," the neurosurgeon pleaded, "let's be safe. You are recovering from a catastrophic life-threatening illness."

"OK. I'll dictate my book and exercise in physical therapy."

Jerry picked up the telephone and called Leon as soon as the surgeon left the room.

"Leon, I'm stuck in the hospital for one more week. Doctor McGuiness says that my ventricles have not shrunk enough."

"Maybe it takes a little more time."

"I hope so."

"What can I do for you?"

"I need you to write a short will that leaves all my assets to Delilah in case something happens to me."

"Sure, that's not a problem."

"Can you send the document to me with Melinda?"

"Sure. I'll have it for you in the morning. Just sign on the dotted lines."

"Also, Leon, I'd like to pay your bill."

"Don't worry, Jerry," Leon insisted. "I've been working on your case pro bono."

"You are most generous, but please, let me send you a check for $1000."

"Sure, Jerry. That will be fine."

Jerry hung up the telephone, picked up his notes then grabbed the small dictating machine.

"Good morning, Melinda," he said into the microphone. "I'm starting the dictation for my book. I'll send you funds after my discharge from the hospital. First, I will be grateful if you would buy a photograph for the front cover. Please call the archives of John Hopkins Hospital, in Baltimore, Maryland. Ask to purchase an image of professor Osler as he examines a patient at the bedside. The man is extending his arm outward. I'll reimburse your expenses. Doctor Osler helped establish the American system of teaching medical students at the end of the nineteenth century. The title page is as follows: THE ROMANCE OF BEDSIDE DIAGNOSIS (in capital letters please). Please place my name several spaces below: JEROME STERN, M.D.

Melinda, Jerry continued, the next page is for dedications. I'm going to use two. First, type in the middle of the sheet the following sentence: For my patients who have inspired me with their trust and courage. Also, add a quote from Sir William Osler, M.D. several spaces below. The following sentence needs to be italicized: *To serve to art of medicine as it should be served, one must love his fellow-men."*—Please place Doctor Osler's name under the quotation.

Next, Melinda, type the words TABLE OF CONTENTS (in capital letters) on the next sheet, and add the list of chapters throughout the dictation. We can fill in page numbers later. OK, let's go. The first chapter is titled, A SECRET CONSULTATION."

Usually, I time my early morning runs to greet the dawn, and while jogging down the empty road, with birds chirping in the trees, the earth slowly gathers light, and soon, the rising sun fills the sky with reddish orange colors that thrills my soul, shielding it from the stresses of my profession.

Yes, medical academic life is a unique challenge since research, lectures, teaching, patient care, writing articles and drafting proposals for grants seem to merge into a single stressful thing that prevents me from finding a period for the end of the day.

But the fluid motion of my legs on the road, watching sunrise and my ritualistic encounter with nature helps me cope—control my life. On this day, however, this dreadful, awful day, a somber mood has suffused my soul. For throughout the night, I've tossed and turned worrying about yesterday's meeting with the chief of medicine. Did he really say that my position at the university seemed in jeopardy?

Quickly showering, and I drove to the hospital where as an assistant professor of medicine, I led rounds for infectious disease fellows, met with a research technician to energize a project in my laboratory then consulted with microbiologists and searched for organisms that might yield interesting cases for an afternoon seminar with students. Following lunch with other members of the faculty, I opened my box in the mail room and received body blows from two letters. One, from editors of the New England Journal of medicine, detailed reasons for their rejection of my manuscript. "Two year of work down the drain," I thought. Next, I opened a letter from the National Institute of Health. Arbitrators had sent two pages criticizing my request for continuing research funds. "They have cut me off," I said to myself. "I'll need to fire my technician and do the work myself."

Distressed, I quickly walked to my office where my mentor sat in a chair waiting for my arrival.

"Jerry," he said, "sit down. We need to talk."

"OK, let's talk."

"I've taken a position at a new medical school in California and must leave immediately. After I'm gone, I don't believe your position in the university will be viable."

"Not viable?"

"No. I'm sorry. I have greatly appreciated your efforts here over the years." He rose from his chair, turned then disappeared down a staircase.

Fleetingly, I hoped for an invitation to join his new challenge, but with rising anxiety, I shut my office door and locked it in anger.

Stunned, feeling like a deer caught in headlights, I became rooted at my desks but eventually rose toward an open window to contemplate my fate. A cool breeze freshened my face, and in the courtyard below, I noted new leaves sprouting from branches and birds chirping everywhere. These signs of new life only deepened the gloom as my dream of becoming a full professor of medicine had become shattered like a glass of champagne striking a marble floor. While happy at the university, I had sensed waning support from the chief of medicine. Yes, publish or perish, the unforgiving rule of academic life, had claimed another victim. "I could write another paper," I thought. "But probably, my body would slowly twist in the wind like a dangling country ham. Only one option seemed available: I had to buy a black bag and practice medicine. For centuries, physicians placed signs outside their offices, waited for illnesses then built practices—one patient at a time. I could do it too."

I tendered my resignation to the university then devoted my efforts in two directions: First, I began searching for a city to hang a shingle, and second, considered ways to retool my brain for everyday medicine. Before long, I snared a temporary position in a tourist clinic on the Maryland shore then began enjoying one month of sun and medicine. Next, I returned to the university to join cardiologists on their teaching rounds. While uncomfortable among the medical students, everyone treated me with respect—they knew my rusty brain needed scraping. Intermittently, I explored advertised positions and one seemed promising in the midwest. Promptly, I flew there and they inspected me during my evaluation of their clinic. While walking through the hospital, my wife, who had developed an ethereal beauty in her third decade of life, attracted many glances from doctors in the hall. But the chief's first words seemed inappropriate and slightly offensive.

"I hear that your wife is a real looker," he said with a smile.

During rounds, the chief confirmed my worst fears as he grabbed nurses on every floor. Quickly, I scratched Peyton Place Medical Clinic from my list, and with time running out, a solo practice seemed like the only available option. Eventually, I flew to a southeastern city, but practicing in four hospitals appeared like a formidable task. During this exploration, however, someone mentioned a city to the west that desperately needed doctors. After a brief inquiry, everything changed as hospital administrators wined and dined us in homes built deep in the woods. For sure, the opportunity seemed ideal since the town had fine schools, a good library, a playhouse, a symphony and a good hospital. In addition, they offered free office rent for six months. Relieved, I agreed to practice in this community.

While finishing the packing, I mused about my new life. "Yes," I thought, "in a few hours, silver wings will lift me into the pale blue sky, away from bitterness and despair." Suddenly, the ringing telephone jarred my nerves, and on lifting the receiver, a friend's voice echoed desperation over the line.

"Before you leave," he pleaded, "will you visit my wife Jane in the hospital? She has double pneumonia."

Driving northward, away from the city, I searched for a small suburban medical center, and on winding tree-shaded roads, my mind became flooded with colliding thoughts of failed academic career, the new life waiting just hours away and the serious illness of an old friend.

"This will not be a social call," I said to myself. "He probably needs a second opinion, but for ethical reasons, I could neither examine Jane nor review her chart. Somehow, someway, I had to render a secret consultation."

I located the hospital, found the patient's room and noticed my friend sitting bolt upright using nasal oxygen. Her husband waited beside the bed.

"Jane, how are things going?"

She breathed heavily trying to answer. "Not good. My chest hurts when I breathe.

I have double pneumonia."

"I see powerful antibiotics in your intravenous fluids. Are they working?"

"I still have fever. I still can't breathe."

41

"Jane, you look bad. Would you mind if I examined you? I have my stethoscope in my pocket."

"All right. I'm sure my doctor has left the hospital."

The skin felt warm; the breathing seemed shallow and labored; and the eyelids looked puffy. The pulse, under my fingertips, vanished with each inspired breath; and when I lowered the head of the bed, neck-veins bulged. The heart, enlarged to percussion, revealed a ventricular Gallup rhythm—a sign of heart failure. The chest expanded symmetrically in my hands but the search for percussion dullness, a sign of pneumonia, proved futile; and over both lung fields crackling sounds flooded my stethoscope. My fingertips detected a tender liver edge and pressure on the legs revealed pitting edema (fluid).

"Jane, pneumonia may be the wrong diagnosis. All signs suggest heart failure and pulmonary edema—that's fluid in the lungs."

"That can't be true. I have double pneumonia. My chest hurts when I breathe."

"The heart is probably inflamed from a viral condition called pericarditis and myocarditis. I'm reasonably sure about this diagnosis since your pulse vanishes with each breath. This sign is called pulsus paradoxus. The paradox is this: The hearts still beats in your chest while the pulse disappears. The sac around your heart, the pericardium, now holds fluid. It is attached to the diaphragm and it's pulled tight like a vise as you breathe. Also, you've developed pulmonary edema—a fatal complication. You must transfer to the university hospital—immediately.

Jane seemed to gasp and became agitated. 'I won't do that. I love this hospital. I love my doctor."

Her husband began weeping, holding his head in his hands.

"I'll be fine," she continued. "Give me a few more days—I'll lick this infection."

"Look, Jane, you're seriously ill and need treatment by an expert cardiologist. I can't call your doctor and announced a new diagnosis. He might file charges against me with the state's medical board. Please

42

try to understand—this examination violated medical ethics. It will be better for you, and for me, if you transfer to another hospital."

I gripped the railings at the end of the bed until my knuckles turned white. "Jane, you're a great professor of mathematics—always searching for perfection. You're the best. But here, the figures don't add up. You're desperately ill in a small hospital but only minutes away from terrific specialized care. Tomorrow, in a place less than perfect, your life might end."

The husband wept continuously and cried: "Please. Please."

"OK, OK, I'll do it. I'll transfer."

I turned to her husband and squeezed her shoulder.

"Call 911—get an ambulance."

"That's ridiculous. You want to extract my wife from this hospital with an ambulance?"

"Yes, do it now—fluid is bubbling through her lungs. A cardiologist will receive her in the emergency room and will I will disappear into the hall. This consultation must remain secret."

Sirens screamed in the courtyard, stretcher-bearers raced through the corridor then burst into the room. "What's going on," a man asked.

Her husband began shouting. "Load her up. Load her up. Take her to the university hospital." The head nurse looked on in amazement. "You can't leave. You don't have permission."

"You bet your sweet-life she's leaving," the husband yelled. "I'll sign the papers. We have the right diagnosis."

I called Jane's cardiologist from the airport and listened carefully to his opinion. "Jane is a courageous patient. I agree with your diagnosis. I've drained fluid from her pericardial sac, injected diuretics and steroids. She'll be fine."

Soon, my airplane gathered speed on the runway then lifted off into a bright blue afternoon sky. Suddenly, my eyes filled with tears as my heart burst with joy. "Perhaps," I thought, "academic medicine has been prologue—just prologue."

"OK, Melinda. That's it. Here is chapter two: A SENSATIONAL DIAGNOSIS.

"I have a rural physician on the telephone," my secretary informed me during a busy afternoon. "He would like to transfer a 17-year-old high school boy who has been suffering with headaches and fever for one month."

"Fever for one month?"

"Yes."

"Put him through on my line. And please, hold all calls."

"This patient has headaches, fever and drenching sweats, "the family doctor said over the line. "I've tried many antibiotics but they haven't worked; and I don't have a diagnsosis."

"A 17-year-old with those symptoms might have infectious mononucleosis," I said. "Have you performed the diagnostic slide test?"

"Yes, it's negative."

"Not many infections last one month," I told him. "Typhoid might cause prolonged fever. Have you cultured his stools?"

"Yes, they're normal."

"What about bacterial endocarditis? Are blood cultures sterile?"

"Yes."

"Brain abscess is a possibility. Does he have a normal scan of the head?"

"Yes, and the spinal fluid is clean, too."

"Tell me about the chest X-ray. Tuberculosis is a possibility."

"Normal."

"Have you checked for osteomyelitis with a bone scan?"

"Negative."

"Do you have malaria down there?"

"No."

"Does he have leukemia?"

"No."

"You have a difficult case. Tell the family to expect a long hospitalization."

"He's too weak to travel by car," the doctor announced. "He'll need an ambulance."

"OK. I'll examine him on arrival."

Several hours later, the boy arrived. I finished treating several patients and my secretary rescheduled others. "What might have caused this strange illness?" I asked myself while walking to the hospital. His parents waited outside the door of the room.

"I've spoken with your family doctor. As you know, tests performed in you local hospital have not yielded an answer. I'll discuss your son's case after finishing the examination."

My heart felt wrenched as I watched the teenage boy shivering with chills, curled in a ball. I tried a light-hearted approach while opening my black bag.

"Well," I asked, "what will you do when you grow up?"

"I'm going to be a veterinarian. Even now, I make rounds on farms with a "vet" after school and on weekends."

"Really! What type of animals do you treat?"

"We inject cattle with vaccine. It's lots of fun."

"Isn't that a live vaccine?"

"I think so."

Quickly, I grabbed the telephone to call the laboratory.

"My patient needs a "stat" serum Brucella agglutination test and three blood cultures." "Please bring those special Castaneda flasks that grow Brucella."

"If this boy has brucellosis, I thought, "this diagnosis might be established immediately, and I'll step out of the room, tell the parents and knock the socks right off their feet. A great case! A sensational diagnosis! Patiently, I waited as the laboratory technician drew blood before starting the physical examination.

The tiny body seemed emaciated; the skin felt hot; and under my fingertips, the pulse bounded at 120 beats per minute. Barely adequate, the blood pressure measured at 90/40 mm Hg. The optic disc looked flat; the neck flexed easily in my hands ruling out meningitis and I detected tender cervical lymph nodes. The heart and lungs revealed nothing of interest but I found a tender liver edge; and under the left rib cage, my hand felt a large exquisitely tender spleen.

"This patient's spleen," I thought, "must be infected like those found in patients described in 1887 by David Bruce who first isolated organisms causing Malta Fever. Studying dead soldiers, he aspirated this organ then observed the fluid swarming with bacteria under the lens of a microscope."

The telephone rang and I lifted the receiver to hear the report from the laboratory. The patient's sera held agglutinins to Brucella abortus at a titer of 1:320.

"Bingo," I thought. "This is a great case—confirmed diagnosis within one hour of hospitalization. Sensational!"

"Well, doctor," said the father, "do you have any clues about my son's illness?"

"I smiled. "He has acute brucellosis. He became infected while injecting live Brucella vaccine into cattle with your local veterinarian. A laboratory test just confirmed my diagnosis. I'll start treatment with tetracycline and streptomycin and his temperature will be lower in the morning. He'll be fine."

"What?" the father angrily yelled. "You've established this diagnosis in a few minutes and my family doctor let my son stay ill for an entire month? I'll kill the man. We'll never use him again."

I heard neither compliments nor gratitude for my terrific diagnosis and felt shocked by the father's rage.

"No! No! No!" I shouted. "You don't understand. "Physicians might practice an entire lifetime and never see a case like this. I've only seen three. Your doctor recognized a rare infection—good judgment, indeed. I'm just an instrument of his practice, doing his bidding—that's all. He's a caring doctor—deeply troubled by your son's illness. I'll start antibiotics and he'll finish treatment in his office. Trust me—you have a fine doctor in your small town."

In the morning, the chart revealed that the boy had a normal temperature and the faces of his parents displayed broad smiles.

"Your doctor is thrilled with your son's diagnosis," I said. "He wants you to stop by his office on your way home."

"I can't wait to show him how good he looks," the father beamed.

As the nurse wheeled the patient toward the hospital's exit, I retreated to a small dictating booth, and with my face in my hands, reflected on the past day's events.

"Why do you lust for great cases?" I asked myself. "You almost transformed a professional triumph into a disaster."

"I'm thrilled to find subtle diagnostic clues—the uplifting joy of medicine," I said under my breath. "This nonsense must stop. If the showman rises again from your soul, remember this patient—the boy with a burning desire to become a veterinarian."

"That's it, Melinda. I'm ready to dictate chapter three. The title is as follows: THE MOST BEAUTIFUL GIRL."

On a winding mountain road, a passing car grazed her leg as she crouched near the ground changing a tire. In a split second, fractured bone sliced through muscle and skin, shifting a 21-year-old life into tragedy, and despite debridement of the wound, the leg developed a dangerous complication—gas gangrene. To save her life, a surgeon recommended amputation of the leg.

While reviewing the chart in the intensive care unit, I watched her move in a small glass cubicle. With long, slow elegant strokes, she combed golden hair over bare bronze shoulders, and like a model drawn by anatomist Andreas Versalias, her arm and neck muscles arched and bulged. Instantly, love pierced my soul like a bolt of lightning bursting through the glass. Here I sat, a physician falling in love with a critically ill patient. "This is incredible and unethical," I thought while trying to suppress my abnormal reaction. "Just incredible. A patient dying of gas gangrene is not sexy. Control your emotions. Go in there and save her life."

Shaken, I approached the secretary at the desk. "Find a nurse to help me examine the patient in bed one. Right now, please."

"I'm, I'm, I'm an infectious disease internist," I stuttered after entering the patient's room. "Your surgeon asked for a second opinion regarding you illness. You're on the tomorrow's surgical schedule. He will amputate your leg below the knee."

"I've never heard of your specialty."

"We're infection detectives who decide about diagnoses and recommend treatments after talking to patients and performing careful physical examinations."

"I have gas gangrene. The leg needs to be hacked off or I'll die. I can feel the gas advancing up my thigh. I don't want it spreading into my belly."

"Where are your parents? Who will help you make this decision?"

"They're dead—I trust my doctor."

"How did you develop those huge arm and leg muscles?"

'I backpack, climb and explore canyons."

"How does a person climb in a canyon?"

"Well, we backpack to a rim, pound pitons into walls to hold our ropes, repel down to the water, strip, load gear in small rubber rafts then float down the river."

"What do you do down there?"

"Oh, we swim, scout, sit under little waterfalls and soak up the sun on red sandy beaches. Sometimes, we lie for hours just watching the water and changing colors in the walls."

"You seem calm about your surgery. May I ask why?"

"I've been on many dangerous climbs. I just suck it up and make the right move for survival. If my leg needs to be cut off—I'll do it."

"Your doctor says he confirmed a diagnosis of gas gangrene. He cultured Clostridium perfringens from your wound. This bacterium produces large quantities of gas as it destroys muscle tissues."

"I know. I know."

"The presence of gas doesn't establish this diagnosis."

"What are you trying to tell me?"

"To start with, you don't look like a victim of gas gangrene. In the Civil War, as you probably know, thousands of soldiers died from this infection. How do you think they behaved on those battlefields?"

"They probably screamed their heads off. But I haven't been shot."

"Yes, they suffered terrible pain but you look quite comfortable. I'll give you my opinion after the examination."

The skin felt warm, not hot; and the pulse, though rapid was not bounding. Only the right leg seemed diseased. In the middle of the thigh, my hands felt crepitations—tiny bubbles under the skin; and gas encased the entire lower leg. A terrible odor filled the room as I removed gauze from the wound. "This is the battlefield-stench of death," I thought.

"Your leg muscles are not swollen." I said while squeezing the muscles of her leg starting with the upper thigh. Slowly, I moved my fingertips down toward her ankle.

"Does this hurt?"

"Not much—it's just a little sore."

"I don't believe you have gas gangrene. Patients with gas gangrene

49

have high fever, extreme pain, severe muscle tenderness and massive swelling of their tissues. A subcutaneous infection, a skin infection, probably released gas into your leg and the dead tissue in your wound needs to be removed—that's all. We call this procedure surgical debridement. Your leg can be saved."

"My doctor says it's my leg or my life."

"We have a split-decision here. Please trust me—cancel the surgery."

"Will I die tomorrow if you're wrong?"

"Yes, you'll probably die."

"I don't want that. I trust my doctor."

"Do you have a boyfriend?"

"Yes. What does that have to do with anything?"

"Please call him right now."

She dialed a number.

"He's on the line."

"Can he be here by six o'clock?"

"He says, yes."

"Ask him if he loves you."

"He says he does."

"Now, tell him that I love you too."

"This doctor says he loves me."

I turned to leave the room. "I'll be back by six o'clock."

Later that evening, I found the patient's boyfriend sitting on the bed holding the girl's hand. "I've spoken at length with your doctor," I told them. "He doesn't agree with my diagnosis. Tomorrow, he intends to amputate your leg. I can't convince him to try the debridement procedure. I strongly advise that you reject the option for amputation."

Tears welled up in her boyfriend's eyes. "The surgeon says she'll die of gas gangrene," he said mournfully. "Anyway, what kind of doctor tells a patient that he loves her?"

"Look. I care about your girlfriend but couldn't communicate. She is terrified by the gas in her leg and I needed to say something to get her attention."

"Doctor, I believe you have her attention. You also have my attention."

"This illness is like one of your climbing experiences," I offered. "You've placed a piton in a loose crack while repelling down a sheer cliff. Now, you must pull it out and pound a new bolt into a solid cleft. You'll need to suck it up to save your leg!"

"I don't know what to do," the boyfriend stammered. "We've climbed together for several years but that's finished. She signed the papers for surgery—it's all set."

"Really? Really? It seems that I can't stop this amputation."

The girl turned toward me and frowned. "Its my damn life and my damn leg."

"I know," I said while looking at the floor. "I'm leaving now. There is little more that I can do. But I'm upset when any patient needlessly loses a leg. In your case, I'm especially sad because hiking and climbing have blessed you with extraordinary athletic beauty. In fact, you might be the most beautiful girl on the face on this earth."

Suddenly, she began a terrible uncontrolled weeping. Her body, as if racked by pain, swayed back and forth with each sob. "I'll try to keep my leg. I'll yank the damn piton out of the damn crack and I'll hammer it into your damn wall. But listen to me, doctor, you better not let me fall."

"Don't worry. I'll tell the surgeon that you'll risk your life to save the leg. It will heal after the wound is cleaned. Trust me. Please trust me!"

Twenty-four hours after the surgery, I found less gas in the patient's leg, little odor in the wound and she smiled during the examination.

"I'm already planning another climbing trip," she said. "Usually, we descend into canyons after dawn and repel into huge purple shadows on the walls. I can't wait to push off from a rim in early morning light. I just can't wait."

"Thank you, Melinda. That's all for the day."

Jerry's telephone rang, he picked up the receiver and heard Delilah's voice on the line.

"Has Doctor McGuinness written your discharge?"

"No," Jerry replied with a low voice. "He plans to observe me here for one more week. He says my ventricles have stopped shrinking."

"What does that mean?"

"I don't know. I'm just going to camp out here, dictate chapters for my book and exercise in physical therapy."

"Why don't you get a pass for this afternoon," Delilah suggested. "I'll drive you to the Bike Zoo and help with the purchase of cycling clothes."

"That sounds great. I'll meet you in front of the hospital in one hour."

Before long, Jerry stepped into a modern bike shop and watched in awe as Delilah began ordering clothes like a drill sergeant.

"Jerry is cycling with me in Europe in six weeks," she told the manager. "He'll need everything. Let's start with a screaming yellow windbreaker. Good. Good. Let's have two bright yellow jerseys. Good. These look good. Now, get him two pairs of bike pants. I want Giordana, they have the best padding. Good. These are good. Next, I want biking underwear. Two pairs."

"What is the purpose of that?"

Padded underwear will protect your crotch," Delilah said with a smile. "Now, let's try on a helmet. We need a strong one because

Jerry has a hole in his skull."

The manager went to a shelf and pulled out a bright red Giro Monza helmet then placed it on Jerry's head.

"How does this feel?"

"Good. Good."

"Now, let's get socks, six pairs and SPD shoes for the clipless pedals."

Jerry tried on the shoes and found a pair with an exact fit. Then, he retreated to the dressing room, pulled on his cycling outfit and emerged looking like a pro.

Delilah smiled. "You look great. But one more item needs to be purchased—a can of bag balm.

Jerry frowned and gave Delilah a half smile, "What is bag balm? Why do I need it?"

Delilah placed her arm around the manager's shoulder. "Would you mind showing Jerry how to use bag balm?"

"No problem. Jerry, come with me. I'm going to show you how to protect your crotch while cycling." He opened a can of bag balm.

"Pull out a plug of this ointment with your middle finger, open the top of your bike pants and place it in the center of your crotch. This material contains an inflammatory drug that softens the teats of cows and helps cyclists too. Believe me, a swollen tender crotch will prevent you from riding. Its extremely painful. Apply the ointment each morning before your ride."

Dutifully, Jerry dug out ointment from the can and placed it in the center of his crotch. He smiled. "This feels good."

The manager grabbed Jerry's arm and pulled him toward his bike.

"Let's put your Trek on a stand and have you mount up so we can teach you how to use clipless pedals.

Promptly, Jerry sat on his new bike.

"Now, thrust the front of your shoe into the cleat. Good. That's good. You are engaged. Now, twist your ankle slightly to the side to release your foot. Good. Good. Engage. Release. Engage. Release. Good. You are doing good?"

"Can you make the release easier?" Jerry asked.

"Sure," he said with a smile. "Just turn the screw with this little wrench until the release is almost effortless. You can do it yourself on the road if you like. But remember. You only have a split second to pull out of the pedal. Otherwise, you will fall on your face."

"Start flipping the gears," Delilah instructed.

Jerry grabbed the drop of the handlebars, cocked his head upwards and began pedaling at a furious pace while changing gears.

"I'm a downhill racer. I'm a downhill racer."

"You look wonderful," Delilah exclaimed. "I can't wait to take you out on the road. Pay for the clothes, Jerry, and let's get you back to the hospital."

Once in the car, Jerry gave Delilah the first cassette. "Please drop this off at the office of Leon Rittenbaum. Ask for Melinda. She's going type my manuscript."

Before long, Jerry was back in his room where an aide snatched him for his exercise in physical therapy. But meanwhile, Delilah was on the telephone with Doctor Terrance Smith.

"Why has Jerry's discharge been delayed?" she asked with some anxiety.

"Doctor McGuinness would have liked more shrinkage of the ventricles," he replied. "Next week, he'll flush out the tube in the brain if the ventricles begin enlarging again. Otherwise, Jerry, will be released. I don't believe there is any reason for great concern. He's back to normal as far as I can tell. He even dictated three chapters of his book from memory."

Delilah sighed with some relief. "We're cycling through Europe in just six weeks."

In the morning, Jerry began sipping coffee while reviewing notes for his book. He picked up the dictating machine. "Good morning, Melinda. I have three more chapters for you today. Let's go. Here is chapter four, A DANGEROUS KISS."

I heard sobs, continuous sobs and felt unsettled on entering the patient's room. A high school girl, hospitalized because of fever and large nodules in both lungs, had become distraught. Her mother waited beside the bed.

"I'm an infectious disease internist," I announced. "Your family doctor asked me to give an opinion."

The patient's mother looked up with a scowl. "The surgeon just left. He's going to perform surgery to biopsy large lumps in her lungs. She doesn't want her chest cracked open."

"Why not?" I inquired as the girl's cries increased into a wail.

"She bought a low-cut gown with thin straps for the senior prom and doesn't want a scar showing at the dance."

"I won't be able to wear a bikini," the girl wimpered.

"Let me talk with the doctor. I'll be back in a few minutes."

Approaching the nurse's station, I found the surgeon writing in the patient's chart.

"Why are you on this case?" he inquired.

"I've been asked to give an opinion. The girl doesn't want her chest opened and she's bawling her heart out."

"Didn't you see those large circular lesions in her lungs? They must be metastatic cancer. We need a diagnosis as fast as possible."

"She also has fever."

"I've seen plenty of cancer patients with fever," he offered. "Also, she hasn't responded to intravenous antibiotics.?"

"She's crying so hard that I can't perform an examination. Can't you wait an extra day to let me finish this consultation?"

"Twenty-four hours, that's all."

The mother still held her weeping daughter when I returned to the room.

After pulling up a chair and holding the girl's hand, I began speaking softly. "Dr. Jones has agreed to a one-day delay of your open lung-biopsy. Settle down so we can talk. I'll need to perform a careful examination."

"OK. I'll try."

"You've had fever for two weeks?"

"Yes."

"Cough?"

"Yes."

"Coughing blood."

"No."

"Headaches and chills?"

"Yes."

"Chest-pains."

"Yes."

"Do you have pets at home?"

"No."

"Do you live on a farm?"

"No."

"Have you visited a farm?"

"No."

"Why are you asking these questions," the mother inquired.

"Farm animals may carry Q fever, a cause of pneumonia," I offered.

"Have you been around anyone with tuberculosis?"

"No."

"Have you been near a sick person?"

"Yes, my boyfriend."

"What was wrong with him?"

"He was coughing."

"Did you kiss him while he was ill?"

"Yes. I think so."

"I see. Please ask him to be here in the morning."

The skin felt warm, the pulse raced under my fingertips and the blood pressure appeared in the normal range. The neck moved easily in my hands and I found a few tender lymph nodes under the jaw. The heart and lungs revealed nothing of interest, red spots appeared on the surface of the abdomen and the liver edge appeared just below the right rib cage, slightly tender.

"Place your fist under your left flank," I instructed. "This will lift your spleen upward toward my fingers."

Sitting on the side of the bed, I placed one hand over the other and then pushed both under the left rib cage. "Take a deep breath, please."

"I feel the spleen tip. The liver and spleen are both slightly enlarged. Your disease involves these organs and the lungs too."

"Cancer?" the mother asked.

"I'm not sure. I'll order a few tests and return in the morning. Please have your boyfriend here by nine a.m."

Restless and worried, I tossed in my bed during the night, and in the morning, returned to the hospital and found the boyfriend waiting in the room.

"You've been sick?"

"Yes."

"Pneumonia."

"Yes."

"Do you live on a farm?"

"No."

"Have you been around anyone with pneumonia?"

"No."

"Do you have pets?"

"No, but my mother has a parakeet."

"Have you played with it?"

"No, but I've cleaned its cage.'

"How long has your mother kept this bird?"

"A couple months."

"You were treated with antibiotics for pneumonia?"

"Yes."

"Which one?"

"Doxycycline."

Slowly, I turned to the mother. Psittacosis is a disease of parakeets that causes severe pneumonia. This germ, half-way in size between a virus and bacteria, is called Chlamydia and may present with lumps in the lungs. Sometimes, a sick patient with psittacosis may pass the infection to a friend by kissing, and this situation might be dangerous and even fatal because the organism gather strength and becomes aggressive after passing through the first human body. I believe this happened in your daughter's case. I'll change the antibiotics to intravenous doxycycline and order a blood test to document this infection. I'm sure your surgeon will delay the lung-biopsy."

"I thought we agreed to a 24-hour postponement," Dr. Jones

stated when I called him on the telephone.

"George, you've known me for years. I need to observe this patient for several more days. I don't believe she has cancer. Trust me. I need more time."

"OK—three more days."

The girl's fever slowly subsided, a serologic test proved the presence of psittacosis, and each, day, I examined her abdomen trying to detect a shrinking spleen.

"Breathe deeply," I asked the girl sitting on the edge of the bed probing her left rib cage. "It's gone. The spleen is gone."

"No surgery."

"No surgery," I echoed.

Suddenly, she grabbed my shoulder, lunged forward and planted a wet kiss on my cheek.

I offered a nervous smile. "Don't worry. You'll soon be well."

Promptly, I left the room and called the hospital's pharmacist. "I need a week's supply of doxycycline for myself. A patient with psittacosis just kissed my face—a dangerous kiss."

"Melinda, that's it. The next chapter five entitled, A YELLOW BLACK MAN."

Dressed in a full-length robe, wearing long beads and sandals, the scholar spoke about the origins of languages and wove together a tapestry of ancient and modern words that suggested the existence of a common tongue in the development of man. Yes, during that evening, long ago, the speaker aroused my intense curiosity and deep admiration. Surprisingly, an illiterate African teenager became a professor of English with a specialty in linguistics. Now, speaking with eloquence, he swayed back and forth behind the podium as coal-black skin glistened under the lights. "For sure," I thought, "a descendant of the Queen of Sheba stands before us and proclaims that magnificent human minds exist everywhere on earth."

Ironically, the search for man's origin brought the speaker out of Africa after the discovery of a three million year-old hominid fossil in Ethiopia. When anthropologists flooded the country, a husband and wife team spotted a teenage waif squatting in the dirt in Addis Ababa.

The wife spoke to her husband, and said, "I need a son. Get me that boy."

We circled around him at the reception. A man who rose from nothingness spoke about the science of language while jiggling beads and wiggling barefoot toes. He seemed like a Biblical character who had entered our modern world by using a time machine.

Several months later, the speaker and I crossed paths again when university police brought an unconscious black man to the hospital with high fever and yellow eyes.

"I have a case of fulminating viral hepatitis the emergency room physician informed me. "He's in hepatic coma. Will you admit him to your service?"

"Of course."

Shocked to my roots, I found the Ethiopian scholar lying motionless under a sheet breathing with slow shallow heavings of his chest.

"This patient has abnormal respirations," I told the nurse. "He's probably going to die. Let's place him in the intensive care unit where we can use a ventilator. Also, ask the laboratory to perform a type and cross match for ten pints of whole blood."

"Ten units?"

"Yes—I'll need them as soon as possible."

The pulse, slowly beating at 45 per minute, worried me considerably but the blood pressure measured in the normal range; and jaundiced eyes stared upward with large dilated pupils. The neck flexed easily in my hands ruling out meningitis, and the head, heart and lungs revealed no other abnormalities. After placing my stethoscope over the lower right rib cage, I percussed the right upper abdomen with a reflex hammer. Tapping lightly, listening carefully, I heard a loud thump as the instrument passed over the lower edge of the liver. Rarely used, this technique of auscultatory percussion detected this organ three centimeters below the right rib margin. "Infection has not collapsed the liver," I thought. "It's enlarged—a good sign. There's hope for the professor."

Soon, the patient's adoptive parents rushed to his side and I recounted my interesting evening with their son, and expressed my profound sadness and deepest regrets.

"Why is he so ill?" the mother asked.

"A virus damaged the liver and it released toxic metabolic products that have suppressed his brain. People from primitive cultures carry hepatitis B virus, but in your son's case, this infection has become dangerous and probably fatal."

"Isn't there some type of treatment?" the father inquired.

"I've administered intravenous steroids to reduce liver inflammation but another therapy exists—exchange transfusions. It's a blood-washing that reduces abnormal chemicals and the virus-load in his body. While many authorities believe this procedure is useless, a few patients have survived."

"Are you willing to use this method?" the mother queried.

"I've considered this approach but waited for your consent."

"Will it work? Will it work?" pressed the father.

"I'll have him up in a few hours."

"Doctor, no jokes at a time like this!"

"I'm speaking truthfully. He might suddenly awaken if toxic substances are removed, but please, restrain your emotions since coma might return after the procedure."

The counter of the sink in the glass-enclosed cubicle held ten units of blood, and nurses, dressed in gloves and gowns, stood ready to handle the virus-laden fluids with extraordinary care. Phlebotomy bags slowly drained the patient's blood, and then, as fast as possible, he received fresh pints through the intravenous line. After the fifth exchange, the Ethiopian moved; and as the seventh bag emptied into his veins, he mumbled.

"Where am I?" he asked during the tenth infusion.

I turned toward the nurse. "I'll need him completely awake. Order four more pints."

"You've been unconscious from hepatic coma," I told the patient. "Your parents are waiting outside the door."

"You may go in now," I instructed the family. "He's alert but don't get your hopes too high."

The following day, the patient walked in the room, his eyes appeared less jaundiced, and now, serum tests revealed a reduction of liver enzymes.

"Is this a permanent recovery?" the mother asked.

"His chances for survival will improve with each passing day."

Gradually, the scholar gained strength, and two weeks later, seemed ready to return home. Once again, the anthropologists arrived to extract their son from the void.

"I'm so pleased that you survived," I said to the patient.

He smiled and extended his hand. "I think you attended my lecture at the university. We met at the reception."

"Yes, my friends and I enjoyed your discussion about the origins of language but everyone felt stunned by your clothes. You looked like the Prince of Ethiopia."

"I'm not a prince. My parents dredged me out of African dust. You're the royal one, my special prince—a prince of medicine."

"Melinda, thank you very much. Chapter six is entitled, BLOODLETTING AT A BIRTHDAY PARTY."

Flashes of blue water and golden afternoon sunlight flickered on and off between the trees as we sped toward the party on a narrow lakeshore road. We approached a house nestled beside a lake.

My wife smiled. "What a gorgeous site for a 50th birthday celebration. This should be an interesting evening."

We greeted Joey with hugs and kisses as pounding rock music echoed in our ears, and while moving around an enormous living room, people jostled us and held drinking glasses high above their heads; and everyone focused their attention on long groaning boards filled with food.

"Happy birthday dear Joey. Happy birthday to you."

Joey, gray-haired and heavy-set, moved with grace and vigor, laughed, cracked jokes and enjoyed his special day. Yes, we loved this man.

"Happy birthday to you. Happy birthday to you. For he's a jolly good fellow, for he's a jolly good fellow—as anyone can plainly see."

We savored delicious food and wine with other guests but unrelenting noise forced us downstairs into a wood-paneled den where long windows exposed the lake's glassy water in the dying glow of twilight. At the end of the room, a brick fireplace, surrounded with pillows, enticed us toward the roaring flames. Soon, relaxed and hypnotized by the blaze, I dozed on and off drifting into a silky envelope of peace. Suddenly, someone grabbed my arm.

"Come quickly. Joey passed out—too much whiskey."

After pushing through the crowd, I reached a narrow pantry where Joey lay crumpled on the floor, semiconscious, breathing rapidly. A dusky blue color mottled his face. The pulse, rapid and thin, revealed a regular rhythm but bubbling noises penetrated my ear as I placed my head on his chest.

"His lungs are filled with fluid—pulmonary edema," I said to men behind me.

"I'll dial 911 for an ambulance," someone yelled.

"There's no time for outside help. Joey will die in a few minutes—it's a heart attack. He'll need treatment here, right now."

"All of you," I shouted, "Help me brace him upright. That's it. Lift his shoulders up against the wall."

"His head's flopping," someone warned.

"Don't worry. Hold him upright. Blood flow to the heart falls by 30% in this position."

"Now give me your belts," I bellowed. "Four belts. Let's trap blood away from the heart. Wrap them tightly around his arms and thighs like tourniquets. Pull hard. Pull hard. Good. Good."

"Now grab a knife from the kitchen," I yelled. "Quick!"

"What the hell are you going to do?" a man asked.

"I'm going to bleed him—execute a phlebotomy. Get the knife—a sharp butcher knife. Didn't you hear me? Get the damn knife!"

"Good. Good. Now bring me a pan."

"Trust me Joey," I whispered while slicing through the skin on top of his wrist. Instantly, veins released squirting blood that created a harsh metallic striking sound in the pan, and rapidly, red liquid filled the bottom of the vessel while music and laughter filtered into the pantry.

"Happy birthday dear Joey. Happy birthday to you."

Gradually, Joey's breathing slowed, blue color faded from his face, but suddenly, he moved.

"Hold him," I shouted. "Don't let him rise—not even an inch. Dump a quart of milk so I can measure the blood. I'll bleed him one-half quart—that's all."

Finally, Joey's wife found us while sirens screamed outside the house.

"He's bleeding. What have you done to my husband?"

"It's a heart attack. This bloodletting removed fluid from his lungs. Please, bring tape to bind his wrist."

"What happened?" Joey asked while trying to rise.

"You developed pulmonary edema after a heart attack—the ambulance will take you to the hospital. I've bled you like a physicians practicing in the Middle Ages. I'm sorry, but I had to cut your wrist. It seemed like the right thing to do."

During the homeward journey, my car hurtled along a blackened shoreline road as the moon's pale light flickered on and off between the trees. Images of the party, the soothing fireplace and the evening's frantic ending all crashed together in my mind, creating a troubled mood. But the lives and contributions of sages, Rene Laennec, Austin Flint, and William Osler entered the ruminations. Somehow, for the first time in my career, I felt worthy of their cherished legacy.

"That's it, Melinda. I'll try to send you this cassette as soon as possible."

A little later, Jerry's telephone rang and he found Delilah on the line. "I've been wondering where you have stored your clothes and bags. Are they still at Heavenly Manor?"

"I don't have any clothes. They transferred me to the nursing home with just the shirt on my back. They expected me to die in a white gown that opened down the back."

"That's ridiculous. Totally ridiculous."

"Don't worry. I need to change my image anyway. You can help me buy some fashionable clothes like those sold by Calvin Klein. I need to dress like an athlete and author. I need jeans, T-shirts, sexy underwear and low boots."

"Meet me outside at one p.m. You can use your new visa card."

Before long, at a store dedicated to selling men's designer wear, Delilah had Jerry fully clothed in a manner fulfilling his new image.

"I really like my low-cut shorts," he said. "I feel young again. Here, deliver this cassette to Melinda."

"When am I going to read some of these stories?"

"Soon, I will be interested in your opinion."

The next morning, Jerry rose early, pulled on new jeans and T-shirt then slipped his feet into a pair of low-cut boots. Carefully, he arranged his notes then grabbed he dictating machine.

"Good morning, Melinda. I have more work for you. Chapter seven is titled, TRUE LOVE."

Each morning, while driving across the river to the hospital, my eyes always followed them on the bridge. An elderly woman with a protuberant belly carried a blue mesh bag and held the hand of her companion. She didn't lead him like a child since they strolled side by side, but she always gripped his hand. In early morning light, they walked on the span even in the heat of summer, in driving rain and in blowing snow; and their clothes never changed except for coats used during inclement weather. Unnoticed, except by those who cared to see, this recurring promenade revealed true love—a fleeting glimpse of true love.

One afternoon, I received an urgent consultation regarding a 70-year-old man who had developed fever following surgery for a perforated duodenal ulcer. The nurse informed me that the patient's wife had asked for me.

"Didn't the surgeon render the consultation?"

"Not really. She demanded an infection doctor for her husband because he has fever and the abdomen might be explored again."

The bag lady held the patient's hand as I entered the room.

"He's dying doc. You've got to save him."

"The nurse mentioned that you sent for me. May I ask why?"

"He has fever."

"I've reviewed his chart and except for an elevated white blood cells, the laboratory tests haven't been helpful; and his portable chest X-ray is perfectly normal. Please wait outside until I finish the examination."

"I'll stay."

"You want to watch me work?"

"Yes."

"OK. I'll explain everything."

"First, he looks bad which suggests a serious illness."

"I know that."

"The pulse, beating at 100 per minute, is another sign of sickness; and the skin is warm—fever."

While placing my hand on his chest I noted, "He is breathing rapidly as you can see. Something has increased his respiration, and his head and neck look normal. Now, I'll check the heart."

After using percussion on the front of his chest and listening with my stethoscope, I said, "The heart appears normal in size and it sounds fine too. I don't believe it's a problem."

"Let's look at his belly," I added while pulling the sheet away. "See, it's badly swollen, tender everywhere and his bowel sounds are faint, too. There could be infection in the abdomen or something else might have slowed his bowels. His legs are fine—no evidence of swelling or tenderness that might suggest blood clots."

"Now, let's examine his chest," I declared as the nurse lifted the patient upright. "Look, my hands are on his diaphragm and the lungs are barely moving. He can't breathe deeply with a swollen belly; and percussion sounds are good too—no signs of pneumonia or fluid. Now, I'm listening to his lungs. Breathe, please, breathe."

"Do you hear anything?"

"Nothing of interest, but there is an additional maneuver that might be helpful while listening to the lungs. It's called auscultation of the lungs in the side positions. Nurse, place him on his left side."

"In this position," I explained, "the lung against the bed becomes partially collapsed which may reveal hidden crackling sounds of pneumonia. This is a new maneuver."

"Breathe, please, breathe. I hear crackles, inspiratory crackles in the left lung behind his heart. Breathe, please, breathe. Absolutely, crackles in his left lung establish the presence of pneumonia. I can't see this infection in the portable chest X-ray because it lies behind the heart. He'll need intravenous antibiotics and breathing treatments to dilate the bronchial tubes. His recovery will take about one week."

"I'm satisfied. Now, I know why he is sick. I liked watching you and I'm glad you are caring for my husband."

"It's my great pleasure to help him. Actually, over the years, I've watched both of you walking on the bridge. Why do you cross so early in the day?"

"We shop and like to watch the sunrise."

Several weeks later, the bag lady and her husband shuffled on the bridge as yellow beams of morning light filtered through the fog. She griped his hand. Slowly, they moved forward—true love on parade.

"That's it, Melinda. Here is chapter eight, NEVER EXAMINE YOUR SECRETARY."

For several days in a row, the office telephone range at exactly nine a.m. My secretary answered, mumbled something over the line then quickly replaced the receiver.

"Who calls so early?" I asked.

"It's my husband. He worries about my driving through the heavy traffic. He thinks I might be killed driving to work."

"Bad news," I thought. "She might quit. To be safe, I'll need to place an ad for a new secretary. Sure enough, several weeks later, my secretary called, resigned over the telephone, and I began sifting through applications. Promptly, I found an experienced person, a super secretary who listed her age at 73 years.

"My secretary quit without notice," I told her over the telephone. "I'm in a real jam. Would you try the job tomorrow? You're hired if you like it."

"Sure, but you must know I'm long in years."

She loved the job and my patients loved her too; and despite her years, she worked like a super secretary; and now, an office disaster became a triumph. But four weeks later, I found another girl sitting with my secretary at the desk. Immediately, they rose together and marched into the hallway, arms locked, hips fused.

"I'm the best secretary in town," she said. "This woman is almost the best. She's my friend, Jane—my gift to you. I'm retiring because of the workload. I'm sure you'll be satisfied."

"You've been lucky for me. I'll hire your friend."

Super secretary told the truth. Jane performed as smooth as glass, worked with a cheery disposition, and once again, good fortune blessed my office. But later that month my former secretary called in the office. "I have pain in the belly. My regular doctor has retired. Will you examine me? I will be most grateful."

"I'm sorry to hear that you're ill. As a rule, I don't treat my secretaries, but in your case, I'll make an exception since you worked here only a few weeks."

The next day, her physical examination revealed a tender sigmoid colon.

"You'll need hospitalization for tests," I told her. "When can you go?"

"Tomorrow."

Everything went smoothly in the hospital and her sigmoidoscopy revealed a normal lower colon..

"You may go to your next examination—the barium enema."

Two hours later, a hospital nurse called me the office. "Your patient developed high fever."

"You have the wrong doctor. I sent my patient to radiology for a barium enema. She's fine—I just examined her."

"That's the one I'm talking about. She looks bad. You'll need to come back, at once."

"Now?"

"Now!" she echoed.

"I shouldn't have examined my secretary," I thought while entering her room. I found her face down, face flushed, mumbling incoherently.

"What is her temperature?" I asked the nurse.

"I've recorded 103.5 degrees."

The pulse, difficult to feel, beat 120 per minute; and lying flat, the blood pressure measured 90/70 mm Hg.

"Please sit her up."

Now, her blood pressure measured 55/30 mm Hg—shock. The upright position revealed a catastrophe for my super secretary—and for me.

I turned toward the nurse with a heavy heart. "This looks like Gram-negative bacterial shock. Somehow, the barium enema released organisms into her blood stream. No one dies after a barium enema, but in a few minutes, my super secretary will be dead if I don't work quickly, perfectly and efficiently."

"Get me an intravenous line and two liters of normal saline. Let's push the fluid in fast—very fast."

"Good. Good."

"She'll need two antibiotics—intraveous amikacin and cefatxime. Quick, call the pharmacy. Stat. I'll need the medications in a few minutes."

"Push it in. Quick. Push it in."

"Now, get steroids," I shouted. "Solumedrol—one Gram intravenously. Stat. Push it in. Good. Good."

"Her blood pressure is still low," I muttered. "Hold that bottle of saline high on the air. Higher. Higher. Roll in the fluid. Roll it in."

Gradually, the patient's sitting blood pressure rose to 90/70 Hg. "Infuse another liter of saline as quickly as you can."

Two hours later my super secretary looked better.

"What happened to me?" she asked speaking normally again.

"You've had a bloodstream infection and shock. I'm thrilled that you've improved. I'll call your husband."

I lifted the telephone receiver with a trembling hand. "This is your wife's doctor. She went into shock after her barium enema."

"Shock? What happened?"

"Infection. She's fine now. Come to the hospital in the morning. I'll explain everything."

"I'll be there. You're sure she's OK?"

"Yes, everything is fine."

The next day, my former secretary waited in the room with her husband.

"Your urine culture grew bacteria," I told them. "Probably, the barium enema released organisms into the blood. The managed care company caused part of this problem since they demanded that I finish tests within 48 hours. Ordinarily, before ordering colon examinations, I would have waited for the report on the cultures of the urine. But this is a hard way to diagnose a bladder infection. At least I've discovered why you had abdominal pain. I'm so sorry you had to go through this illness. You might have died yesterday morning since bacterial shock has a mortality rate of 70%."

"Don't worry. I'm sure other doctors would have ordered a colon examination but the nurse told me that you made the diagnosis by measuring my blood pressure sitting upright. I had the right man. Also, I need to tell you how much I enjoyed those four weeks in your office."

"I appreciate your confidence. You are a super secretary and a super human being as well. I love you dearly."

"We're having lunch at a fancy restaurant to celebrate her recovery," the husband announced. "Please join us."

"Thank you very much, but I have an urgent errand. Here is your prescription for antibiotics. See me in two weeks."

In a copying center near the hospital, the computer operator printed a few words in bold three-inch type then placed the sheet into a plastic frame. Then, I returned to my office and hung special words on the wall behind my desk: NEVER EXAMINE YOUR SECRETARY.

"Melinda, I have one more chapter today. Chapter nine is entitled, THE BITE OF THE TICK. Here we go."

"Your new consultation has tick bites, high fever and looks deathly ill," a hospital nurse informed me. "I don't know why anyone would hike in the Great Smoky Mountains National Park."

"That's an interesting place," I replied while flipping pages in the patient's chart. "It's different each season. In summer, breathing and hiking are difficult when heat releases gases from the vegetation, and of course, ticks are everywhere. In the fall, trees become towering masses of colorful leaves and the trail becomes exciting when thunder and lightning burst above your head. Winter is also special, since you crunch on virgin snow while climbing beside roaring streams; and if you're lucky, you see frozen fog covering the bushes and trees, a white-laced wonderland of hoarfrost. Spring, however, may be the best time for trekking to Mount Le Conte because cool mists swirl through the woods moistening your face, and on the summit, above all the vapors, clouds dash in and out between the peaks. One moment everything is revealed, then suddenly, the mountains are hidden under white blankets of cotton candy. And while resting on the cliff, you watch the dying of the day as a huge fireball sits on the earth coloring land and sky in shades of red and gold. Before long, purple shadows race through valleys like giant birds of prey, cold wind rushes in and darkness grips the mountain. Then, with regret, you struggle down a blackened trail for an evening's meal at the lodge."

I opened the door to the patient's room and found it completely still. In the darkness, a beside lamp beamed a downward circle of gloom as a woman stared upward toward the ceiling, immobile. Her chart revealed a temperature of 104 degrees.

"Are you paralyzed?"

"I have a terrible headache. It hurts to move—even an inch."

The pulse felt rapid, the blood pressure fell low in the sitting position suggesting a critical illness; puffy fluid surrounded the eyes, fingers and legs; and the buttocks revealed angry tick bites.

"Do you have a diagnosis?" the husband asked when I left the room.

"She has Rocky Mountain spotted fever. This is a Rickettsial disease, and she became infected from tick-bites while hiking in the mountains. I found classic signs of this infection—headache, high fever and edema—fluid under the skin. I'll treat her with intravenous steroids to block the toxicity of the infection and chloramphenicol to kill the organism. She'll be better in the morning."

"Doctor, that's a pretty cocky answer. She doesn't have any spots."

"A rash doesn't establish this diagnosis, but edema is a vital clue. Also, I found low blood pressure in the sitting position, which proves the presence of a desperate illness. At this stage, laboratory tests will not be helpful. Please, try to understand, for centuries, physicians established the cause of infections by using only physical examinations. Trust me, I'm sure about this diagnosis."

On rounds the next day, the patient's chart revealed a normal temperature and I found her sitting beside a window eating breakfast.

"My headaches are gone," she announced.

"Young lady, you were quite ill last night. Tick-bites caused this infection."

"Doctor, I know what happened, but I'll trek through those beautiful mountains again. Last week, I walked beside streams with cascading water; hiked between towering walls of flowering rhododendron; and on the peak, lingered on the rocks until sun vanished from the sky."

"That's it," Melinda. I might have more for you in a few days or next week. I thank you very much for your help."

Doctor Terrance Smith entered the room and asked, "How are

you doing, Jerry?"

"I'm fine. Yesterday, I bought some new clothes and I'm dictating chapters for my book to Melinda. She is one of Leon's secretary's."

"Jerry, please say for me the following statement: Around the rugged rock the rapid rabbit ran."

Promptly, Jerry stood up and smiled. "Around the rugged rock the rapid rabbit ran."

"That's good. I'm sure you'll be discharged in a few days."

"I can't thank you enough for the accurate diagnosis in my case," Jerry said with tears welling up in his eyes. "You've saved my mind and my life."

"De nada, as they say in Spanish. De nada."

Doctor Smith promptly turned, left the room as Jerry picked up the telephone to call Delilah.

"I can't wait to get out of here. Let's do something in the afternoon."

"OK, we'll work on your bike on an isolated road beside a lake. We can adjust the heights of your seat and handle bars. They will need to be in perfect positions once we start training. Also, you'll need to practice placing your feet in and out of the pedals so you won't fall on your face. Remember, you have a hole in your skull."

"That's great, pick me up at one p.m."

Chapter Nine

THE TRAINING

Several days later, after receiving an excellent report from Doctor McGinness, Jerry dressed, packed his bag then walked out of the hospital into the late afternoon sun. He felt elated but physically spent. Earlier, therapists has pushed his body to its limits. "I'm going to collapse," he had told them. Now, while waiting on the hospital's steps, he reflected on his miraculous recovery. He had been extracted from Heavenly Manor by a beautiful nurse, a neurologist correctly diagnosed his condition, a neurosurgeon drained enlarged ventricles in his brain and his memory returned. Soon, Delilah would arrive to transport him into a new life that opened with an exotic cycling journey in Europe. "Why me? Why have I been saved? For what purpose?"

Jerry saw the van then ran to the curb shouting, "I am going to live. I'm going to live."

Delilah smiled. "Get in Jerry. You are looking alive again."

The little van slowly wound its way through heavy traffic, and eventually, it reached Delilah's small bungalow where Jerry found himself instantly comfortable.

"I'll show you to your room," she said. "Come. Come."

Promptly, they entered a small space enclosed on three sides by glass walls.

"This place used to be a porch. My grandmother closed it in to watch the deer wandering among the trees. Shall I pull the curtains?"

"No. I want to see animal life in the garden and it will be nice to have the sun wake me in the morning. Delilah, I'm really tired and must sleep for awhile. I've had a long hard day and feel emotionally wrenched."

Jerry slipped off his shoes, climbed onto the bed, pulled a knitted blanket around his shoulders, and then, almost instantly fell asleep as

Delilah closed the door.

The sun disappeared and night crept into the room like a silent jungle cat. Suddenly, Jerry sat bolt upright, disoriented in the darkness. He heard the faint delicate sounds of Mozart's flute concerto as shafts of moonlight filtered through the trees entering the room like dim searchlights. Delilah stood in the doorway, immobile. Long auburn hair spilled over her shoulders as faint yellow beams shimmered on her white gown. She moved toward Jerry, slid under the blanket, lifted his shirt and began kissing his chest. Quickly, he grabbed her body saying, "Are you Sampson's Delilah?"

"No, silly. The surgeon buzzed off all your hair. There's nothing left to cut."

Delilah broke into uncontrollable laughter as Jerry slipped off his clothes. In a flash, Delilah felt heat in her pelvis that spread upward into her belly, her chest and then into her throat making it almost impossible to breathe. She curled the heels of her feet around Jerry's back and cried. "Oh. Oh. Jerry. Jerry."

In the morning, Jerry awoke to find half his body and one leg on top of Delilah and felt thrilled with the sensation. He whispered in her ear. "I held you all night long."

"I know. I can barely breathe. Get up and pull on our cycling clothes. A long hilly ride awaits us after breakfast."

"Climbing?"

"Yes, it's only a two hour ride but it's tough. Let's eat and go."

The fog, barely lifted, retreated toward the rivers as Jerry and Delilah cycled on a road that began rising, almost immediately.

"Don't get too close," Delilah yelled. "We don't want to crash."

The road became steeper and Jerry began breathing hard.

Delilah instructed: "Use your easy gears. Don't wear yourself out."

Jerry fell far behind Delilah but kept her in sight. Soon, they arrived at the summit of a long hill, and far below, a green valley and low mountains spread out before their eyes.

Delilah put her arm around Jerry's shoulder. "Isn't this view gorgeous? On the descent, squeeze your brakes on and off. If the rims of your wheels overheat, the tires might explode. I don't want to lose you after all we've been through at the hospital. Be careful. Be careful."

They tilted their bikes downhill, clicked shoes into pedals and slowly began to descend.

"Are we climbing this monster hill on the way back?"

"Sure. That's how we're training for Prague and beyond."

Faster and faster, sweeping through the curves, Delilah and her patient sped toward the beautiful green lowlands and quickly reached a small flat area where they rested cooling their wheels.

"I don't see how we'll climb this hill on the return."

"Don't worry. We'll take it slow. Let's have some coffee at that gas station up ahead. Then, we'll head home."

Before long, Jerry and Delilah began an agonizing ascent, but finally, in late morning, they reached their starting point.

"Let's shower and eat lunch," Delilah suggested.

"Can I shower with you?"

"Not this time. I'm washing my hair."

Jerry showered, dressed in a T-shirt and jeans then retreated to the sofa to arrange his notes for dictation. Before long, Delilah brought sandwiches and drinks to the coffee table.

Jerry rubbed his stomach. "This food is wonderful."

After lunch, Delilah thrust her back against Jerry and smiled. "Tell me a story."

Jerry slipped a hand underneath her shirt.

"Be careful, Jerry, I have a short fuse."

"This chapter is about the problem of seductive female patients and how physicians deal with this difficult situation.

"Office sex?"

"Of course not."

"I don't like this subject. It's dangerous. The state might revoke your medical license. Ha. Ha."

"It's already gone," Jerry stated with a grimace. "Remember?"

"Just kidding."

"Look. Patients frequently use doctors who like them, but there is a difference between liking and loving. Sometimes, for their own reasons, female patients step over an invisible line and become seductive. Most don't really wish to seduce their physicians, but believe me, it's a huge disturbance in the doctor's relationship with the patient. A long time ago, a woman said to me, "Doctor, you raise my blood pressure every time I see you." I didn't react and became cold as ice. Usually, however, the seductiveness is nonverbal, but its equally dangerous and disturbing.

On the other hand, physicians are not potted plants as they examine patients. We are human, like beauty and hate ugliness. Controlling our emotions, however, is part of being a physician. And yes, extending warmth and affection, crossing over the line, sometimes helps the healing process."

Jerry looked at his notes and continued. "Once I had a young female patient who had a tumor of the upper thigh that had ruptured through the skin and extended into the lower pelvis. It was a terrible situation for the patient and doctors, but she acted overtly sexy. I reacted with warmth and held her hand. She desperately needed to know that she was still beautiful. Anyway, I felt it was important to write about this interesting subject."

"What it the title?"

"An awkward attraction," Jerry announced while picking up the dictating machine. "Good morning, Melinda, this is Jerry again with chapter 10. The title is AN AWKWARD ATTRACTION. Delilah thinks this subject is dangerous and it might place me in jeopardy. I would like your opinion. Also, ask Leon if he will read this chapter. I'll remove it if he thinks he might cause a lawsuit. Here we go."

I entered the examining room and closely observed an exotic appearing woman with bronze skin and close-cropped hair. Her thin face projected innocence.

"How are you today, doctor?" she inquired.

"I'm fine," I said feeling nervous and uncomfortable. "The chart lists your age as 50 years. Is that correct?"

"Yes, but marathon runners always look young. I can't race anymore because of dizziness. I hope you can help me. You have a reputation as a great doctor."

"Please follow me to my office to discuss your problem in detail."

"She must look like poetry in motion in a marathon race," I thought as her long-legged body glided through the corridor like a cat."

"You have a beautiful office, doctor. I'm grateful for this prompt appointment since I'm dizzy after starting my morning work-outs."

With twinkling eyes and a wry smile, she twisted back and forth in the chair and except for complaints about mild headaches and dizziness, offered no clues to explain her illness. During the examination, a normal blood pressure rose moderately high in the standing position; and a roaring sound, a bruit, penetrated my ears after placing my stethoscope on the abdomen. The smell of her perfume drove me crazy.

"Your blood pressure rises when you stand," I told the patient. "Also, I hear a musical sound in your belly that may indicate a blocked renal artery. I've ordered a few tests. Come back next week for your reports."

"If she became well," I mused. "we could dangle our feet together in fast-flowing mountain streams."

"I'm so grateful for your help. You're a great doctor."

"Whoa. I haven't solved your case. One of these tests is for menopause since low estrogen-levels might cause vascular instability and another is a kidney X-ray. These tests might suggest the need for additional procedures."

Fascinated, I watched her slither down the hall with long, graceful strides, and that afternoon, struggled through the schedule as her image filled my mind; and the next day, the secretary announced that my marathon runner was one the line.

"I can't thank you enough for your efforts, she said. "I gave blood and performed the kidney X-ray. I can't wait to get the results. You're a wonderful doctor."

"Does she know?" I asked myself. "Had she read my mind? Did I hide my emotions?"

"Hold on. I appreciate your compliments but I haven't found the cause of our high blood pressure."

Her gentle voice threw me into confusion. Feeling shaken, I left for the doctor's lounge in the hospital trying to pull myself together. Yes, this patient bothered me. What caused my unethical reaction? Had she been on the make? I'm not sure, but her natural beauty and sensual movements have driven a deep wedge in my soul. Perhaps, I might find guidance and solace from the Hippocratic oath hanging on the wall.

'With chaste and with holiness, I will pass my life and practice my art. Into whatsoever house I enter, I will go for the benefit of the sick, and will abstain from every voluntary act of mischief and corruptness; and further from any act of seduction to female or male, or free man or slave.'

"Good words," I pondered, "but I feel overwhelmed by this patient."

Next week, she returned to the office and I found her standing blood pressure rising. Once again, she wore the same perfume. "If she recovers, we could climb mountain peaks and watch beautiful sunsets," I thought.

"Your tests revealed a small right kidney," I said. "I've ordered a renal arteriogram. A radiologist will place a catheter into the femoral artery of your leg, thread it up the aorta in the abdomen then squirt dye into the renal arteries."

"Let me think about it. I don't want my legs stuck with needles."

"Take me out to the track," I dreamed. "I'll watch you run. Those long limbs must look gorgeous at full stride."

Yes, trouble gripped my soul: This patient needed a diagnosis but my thoughts threatened my practice, my career and my marriage.

Two days later, I received a call from the emergency room's physician. "Your patient is here with a severe headache and high blood pressure. She's a runner—a marathon runner."

I raced to the lower level of the hospital and found the patient's blood pressure high—sky high.

"Nurse," I cried. "I need an intravenous line for blood pressure medication. Quick, get a line."

"The rise of your blood pressure with standing and running suggest a diagnosis of renal artery stenosis," I said. "You'll need an arteriogram, and if blockage is found, the radiologist can correct it with a balloon-dilation of the artery—right now." The patient put her head down and smiled. "Let's do it."

"Get well. Get well," I silently pleaded. "I'll take you to Europe for the summer where we can hike through the Alps visiting great mountain resorts like Chamonix in France, Grindelwald in Switzerland and Innsbruck in Austria."

"Wow. I feel great. Those blood pressure drugs are wonderful. You've solved my problem. You're a great doctor."

I felt lost—seduced without an act of seduction. Now, my practice seemed irrelevant, but I knew one person who might help me—my old friend, Dr. Nat Cohen. Over the years, he must have experienced attractive seductive patients. Grabbing the telephone, I spoke to his secretary: "Tell Dr. Cohen that I'm coming to see him. I need his help—now."

"Nat," I said, "my personal and professional life are in jeopardy."

Sitting before his desk, I slowly revealed my wonderful obsession, blow by blow.

"I've seen this type patient before," he said. "They're seductive without saying one word. Probably, she behaves the same way with all doctors. Do you think she pines for you at night?"

"No."

"She hungers for an older doctor. Right?"

"No."

"You've made a pass at her?"

"No, but I think she knows."

"Of course she knows. She's watching you react. Have you made a diagnsosis?"

"Yes, renal artery stenosis."

"Then you've wrapped up the case?"

"Yes."

"OK. Your nurse will put an end to this nonsense. Just ask her to hold the patient during the examination. I'll bet you a dinner that she behaves differently."

Two days later the patient returned for her last office visit.

"Doctor," my nurse yelled from the examining room, "we're ready."

I recorded a normal blood pressure in the standing position while my nurse tightly squeezed the patient's arm.

"Everything is fine. I'm sure your dizziness has disappeared."

The patient glued her eyes to the floor. "Yes, I'm better."

"Come back next year for a follow-up examination," I said while quickly exiting the room. I walked to my office, slumped in a chair and sank into a swirling cloud of relief. "What a horrible experience, I thought. "If I see a patient like this again, I'll behave in a cold manner—like a block of ice. Yes, like a block of ice."

"OK, Melinda. That's it. Tomorrow, I'll send you this cassette."

Jerry turned to Delilah. "Well, did you like it?"

"I don't like it. It's risky. This subject is taboo! Let's go to town. I need to pick up maps for the Czech Republic, Austria, France and Tuscany."

"Good idea. I need to stop at the bank to get checks for Leon and Melinda. Did you pay for my flight to Prague?"

"Yes."

"I'll get cash to pay you back. Leon has made me self-sufficient."

Later that evening, Jerry grilled steaks in Delilah's small garden."Where are we going tomorrow?"

"It's a long route of 50 miles without many hills."

"That sounds good. By the way, I want you to sleep in my room tonight. We can watch the sunrise together."

The next day, Jerry enjoyed a flat 50 mile ride with Delilah and didn't feel overly taxed.

"I'm improving. I'm sure with several more weeks of training my body will be ready for cycling in Europe. Where is the next challenge? What type of ride are you planning?"

"Tomorrow's ride will be difficult. We'll combine the first day's hilly route with another 50 miles."

"You're joking."

"No. But you'll receive a real treat since the ride passes beside beautiful farms and a trout pond with a restaurant. It has a real grist mill. You'll love it."

Jerry showered then examined his notes beside the sofa while waiting for Delilah to bring lunch. Before long, they enjoyed their meal and Delilah stretched her legs out over Jerry's lap as he prepared to dictate.

"Jerry, tell me a story."

Jerry slid his hand under her warm-up suit and began caressing her leg.

"Be careful, Jerry. What will you dictate this afternoon?"

"This is a controversial subject that concerns the incorporation of friends into a doctor's practice."

"Isn't it difficult and risky to treat your friends? What happens if you make a mistake? What would you do if one died? How would you feel? Why did you do it?"

Jerry grimaced and began speaking in a low voice. "Delilah, the gist of the matter is this: I needed to display my craft. Look, painters place their canvases on walls for everyone to admire. I felt proud of my skills, and, yes, shamefully, solicited many friends. But please, listen to the stories before you pass a harsh judgment."

"Good morning, Melinda," Jerry said into the machine. This is chapter 11, WHEN FRIENDS BECOME PATIENTS."

Abby, an old friend grabbed my arm at a crowded party. As a physicist in a national laboratory, she investigated the sun's interior by smashing together high-speed metal ions in a cyclotron; and many believed she would win the Nobel Prize.

"I'm thinking of becoming a patient," she said. "I'm worried about my blood pressure—it's sky-high.

I searched for the pulse while shaking her hand.

"Your blood pressure can't be too high since this artery is easily compressed."

"You're measuring my blood pressure with your fingertips?"

"The tension in the artery's wall gives me a rough estimate of the pressure. Please, ask my secretary to schedule your visit as soon as possible."

Later in the week, Abby arrived in my office with a chart of blood pressure readings that appeared extraordinarily high (230/100 mm Hg.). After the examination, she placed powerful medications on my desk.

"My family doctor couldn't help me—even with all these drugs."

"During my examination, your blood pressure measured only 140/90 mm Hg. Please, stop your drugs so I can develop an accurate perspective on your case."

"I'm not going to do that. I'll have a stroke if my blood pressure soars higher."

"Look, I'm an old friend; and now, I'm your doctor. You'll get your money back if there's brain damage."

"That's not funny."

"Please, put these medicines aside and I'll make a house call in the morning. Nothing terrible can happen while your blood pressure is closely monitored."

In her home, I recorded a blood pressure of 140/90 mm Hg.

"This reading is still borderline. Please stand up. Now, it's normal—130/80 mm Hg. Did you stop those drugs?"

"Yes."

"See, you didn't have a stroke—but I'm puzzled. Your own blood pressure measurements don't match my results. Please, take a reading with your machine."

"This blood pressure apparatus is defective," I said after she recorded a high reading. "You don't have hypertension."

"All right—I believe it."

"Come back to the office next month, and please, throw away this gadget."

Should physicians gather friends into their practices? Definitely, yes. But while I"ve enjoyed this interesting task, frequent worries caused sleepless nights. Early in my career, I traded jokes with friends in the office, but this activity felt inappropriate in context of serious illness, and soon, the laughter faded. I loved these patients, turned heaven and earth to resolve their problems, and for sure, their presence in my practice provided a stimulus to work toward perfection; and failure seemed an unthinkable nightmare. While most patients received one hour examinations, I reserved two hours for friends which enabled me to work slowly, and this prolonged sleuthing sent a message: I care.

At social gatherings, friends casually discussed their medical problems and pride might have been a factor when I responded to their queries with confident recommendations; and sometimes, my statements seemed like flashing spinners in the water that hooked desperately hungry fish. On the other hand, I felt concerned that my voice might have been a siren's song luring Odysseus-like individuals toward an island of destruction. But as each success became an affirmation of my art, it seemed that I had lifted the bar impossibly high and continuously worried that false cockiness might bring everything down—doctor, patient and my position in a social circle. Yes, like a moth, I flew close to the flames but enjoyed the danger. At times, however, I had the proclivity to act like a hero. For example: Sometimes, I asked friends to discard drugs prescribed by other doctors to design treatments that would be mine alone. Thus, I might have behaved like a species of squid that flushes out a rival's sperm before mating with a female. Often, to prevent errors, I asked friends to return for extra office visits, and certainly, they never knew how many times I have been awake at night worrying about decisions. Somehow, I felt attracted to the risky nature of these relationships—like sky diving without a backup parachute. I had chosen a special endeavor—gather friends as patients, solve their difficult medical problems, perform error-free, become a hero, control emotions and manipulate interactions. Yes, I felt intoxicated by the challenge.

Why did these individuals join my practice? Well, by definition, friends stand together through thick and thin, and after I saved a few lives, others had incentives to become my patients. In addition, there had been the "V.I.P." issue. What type of patient lifts up the telephone and then becomes a celebrity? Really, it is only the doctor's friend who enjoy this special status—the easy access, the long office visits and the excellent care. They understood that I couldn't afford to make an error and my thorough examinations gave them confidence.

On the negative side, the issue of privacy hung darkly over relationships, and for some, the loss of secrets precluded their entrance into my practice. For others, however, the resolution of illnesses became their only goal. Usually, I had been scrupulously closed-mouthed about discussing a friend's cases with anyone, but on occasion, because of stressful situations, my wife learned about these illnesses. Doesn't a doctor who lies awake at night need to relieve the tension? Yes, indeed! Often, my wife said the right thing: 'Dear, it will turn out all right.'

Sexual issues have been tightly interwoven with questions of patient's privacy, and I usually avoided this subject with my friends, but on occasion, such discussions destroyed fragile medical relationships. This problem became more difficult when caring for females. Should women become patients of a male physician after years of socializing at parties. Probably not! Yet, troubling situations did develop when four entered my practice. One fired me on the spot when I couldn't establish a diagnosis; another, doing poorly, slammed the phone down and left my practice; and a third came to my side of the desk one afternoon. Not understanding her intentions, I quickly told her that she needed care by other physicians. The fourth spoke of her illness in such bizarre terms that I sent her to a university medical center for evaluation and treatment. I did, however, treat a few female friends who swept aside all other concerns and these cases gave me great satisfaction. An old acquaintance, an accomplished senior tennis player, entered my office complaining about rib pains during her matches.

"You probably pulled a muscle in the chest," I told her after the examination. "To be safe, you'll need a stress test—an exercise cardiac evaluation."

I called the cardiologist who performed the procedure after the appearance of slight changes in the electrocardiogram. "Is it safe to send this patient home?" I asked with considerable concern.

"Sure. I'll do a heart catherization next week. She'll be fine."

After instructing the patient to rest at home, a constant worry filled my mind.

"Did your wife arrive?" I asked her husband over the telephone.

"No. she's watching tennis in the park."

Later in the day, she called informing me about her constant rib pain.

"Call 911. Come to the emergency room immediately."

"Promptly, surgeons by-passed blocked coronary arteries saving her life. Apparently, the Grim Reaper had pulled her toward the abyss, dragged one foot across the rim, but I snatched her back by listening to the echoes in my mind.

One morning, a dermatologist called me in the office. "I performed a skin biopsy on the leg of one of your friends. It reveals blastomycosis. Can you see her today?"

"Sure. Have you informed the patient that she has a fatal disseminated fungal infection?"

"That's why she wants to see you."

Quickly, I rearranged my afternoon schedule to evaluate a patient who had been a friend for 20 years.

"My dog had blastomycosis," she told me after arriving in my office. "My veterinarian cured the animal with itraconazole, a new antifungal medication. I guess I'll need that drug, too."

"You probably became infected from a small bite on your leg since this fungus resides in your dog's lungs."

After the examination, I placed her in front of my desk to discuss my findings and the options for treatment.

"I'm going to ask you to perform a chest X-ray, a CT scan of the chest, serum tests for your immune and liver functions," I told her.

"Your liver is slightly enlarged which suggests that this fungus might have spread throughout your body. I might not be able to use itraconazole because liver failure has been reported with this drug. Ketoconazole, another effective medicine, might also damage your liver. On the other hand, use of intravenous Amphotericin B will partially damage your kidneys. Come back tomorrow and I'll decide after inspecting the results of your tests."

"Cancel the rest of today's patients," I told my secretary.

"The schedule is full. Why?"

"I think this last case will be a problem. I can feel it in my bones that something will go wrong. I'll need to review the latest articles on the treatment of blastomycosis. Call me in the medical library."

The librarian ran a computer search for articles, and soon, had key publications faxed to her desk. While itraconazole appeared to be effective for blastomycosis, several reports described patients with drug rashes, hepatitis and liver failure. "I might cause a calamity with the use of itraconazole," I thought, "and I'll need to make a decision by morning." But that night, I tossed and turned in bed and decided to use Amphotericin B. The following day, I found my friend standing in front of the secretary's window with an X-ray file under her arm.

"You're early for your appointment," I told her.

"I'm gathering my medical records. I only trust my family doctor. He'll decide about my treatment. Anyway, I want that medication that cured my dog."

"It looks like I've been fired without giving an opinion."

She lowered her head and looked at the floor. "I'm more comfortable elsewhere."

Immediately, a wave of relief swept over my body as she left the office.

While discussing the difficulties of the friend-physician relationships, I feel compelled to mention another issue. Two individuals complained that I had overcharged them after they received their "V.I.P."

examinations. What type of people would make such ungrateful comments? Probably, those who enjoyed inflicting pain. They found other doctors, and when we met on social occasions, I became quite cool, indeed.

Over the years, serious diseases stalked my friends like mountain lions on the hunt, but their trust in me influenced their decisions to become patients. One developed severe fatigue before departing for vacation, and his wife called to say that he looked bad. While he didn't report chest pain, coronary artery disease seemed a reasonable diagnosis. He rejected my advice, but I mentioned he might "drop dead" if he didn't follow my instructions. Soon, surgeons by-passed five blocked coronary arteries. During a routine physical for another friend, I found ventricular tachycardia—a condition that frequently converts into fatal ventricular fibrillation. Still, another close buddy, in his mid-sixties, called from an out of town hospital where doctors diagnosed heart failure. After the examination, I found a badly leaking mitral valve, but after hospitalizing this man, and while trying to decide the safest course of action, mutual friends pleaded with him to fly to a university hospital for excellent medical care. Upset, I rammed a police car while leaving the hospital. In this case, I carefully weighed the pros and cons of sending him elsewhere since I would have felt devastated if he died on my watch. But in the end, I decided to hold him on my service because of the challenge. Immediately, surgeons replaced the mitral valve and the heart failure disappeared.

One friend, a physician who hospitalized me several years earlier, became one of my most difficult patients. For weeks, I had watched him walking slower and slower through the corridors of the hospital. Then, on a whim, I entered his office offering to measure his blood pressure. Nothing more developed since I assumed another doctor had his case. But later in the week, my secretary informed me that he had called complaining about chest pains. Usually, patients with these symptoms race for emergency rooms. While touched that he gambled everything so that I might admit him to the hospital, I felt shocked with the results of my examination at his desk. Here, I found angina pectoris, heart failure and atrial fibrillation, a serious irregular heart rhythm. Soon, surgeons by-passed coronary arteries, but unfortunately, he suffered a difficult post-operative course.

Each day, I worked slowly and carefully checking his appearance, mental alertness, pulse, blood pressure, heart, lungs and legs. Yes, serious abnormalities appeared including confusion, low blood pressure, heart failure, renal failure and a massive pleural effusion (fluid in the chest). Gradually, these problems resolved but he started smoking again, and I explained that the coronary grafts might clot if his lethal habit didn't stop; and each day, these discussions became tense. Finally, while preparing to leave the hospital, he informed me that another doctor would take over his case.

"Fired?"

"I guess so," he said while turning his face away from me.

How can I summarize the merits of the friend-physician relationships? Well, it can be satisfying but it's often stressful. Frequently, however, it's fun and a great challenge. Overall, I've felt joy working with these patients, trusted my instincts and depended on my art of bedside medicine to resolve illnesses. I had played a high stakes poker game and enjoyed the risks. Yes, I surely did.

"Well, Delilah did you like this last chapter? Was it proper for me to gather friends into my practice?"

"I liked it but you're using this chapter as a confessional. You sound too arrogant and cocky. By the way, how have you been able to spit out this material as if its ready for print?"

"I spent four years laboring over this book and many chapters were rewritten 20 times. But during my illness, my wife destroyed the manuscript. She thought I would die in the nursing home. I know all the words, sentences and even the places for punctuation. I hope Melinda puts the paragraphs in the right position. If not, I'll do it when she gives me the fresh typed pages. I have one more chapter tonight. It concerns sick physicians and the problems they face when they become patients."

"That sounds interesting."

"Good morning, Melinda. Here is chapter 12. The title is as follows:

WHEN DOCTORS BECOME PATIENTS. Here we go."

Exhausted, I arrived home late one evening in a rainstorm and found my telephone ringing.

"Oh God," I thought, "this must be an emergency call."

"I'm sorry to bother you," a local orthopedic surgeon said over the line. "But my patient, a physician, developed a wound infection after lumbar disc-resection. Can you examine her tonight? She's a local psychiatrist."

"Of course. Give me a few minutes to clean-up."

"This sounds like an old sad story," I mused. "Bad things happened when doctors became sick. One colleague, a surgeon, nearly bled to death after a routine hysterectomy; another died from a ruptured cerebral aneurysm after receiving aspirin for headaches; and a third, died in his car after cardiologists failed to press for emergency surgery on his coronary arteries. Physicians frequently medicate themselves, and as professor William Osler stated, 'a physician who treats himself has a fool for a doctor.' For a variety of reasons, physicians feel uncomfortable becoming patients of their associates; and worse, they manipulate them with denial. Also, treating physicians may become nervous and either suggests that complaints are trivial or aggressively order hundreds of tests searching for all possible diseases. Unfortunately, physicians have difficulties becoming just another patient."

For myself, I found medical help with only marginal results. While teaching and developing gastritis (inflammation of the stomach) doctors couldn't stop the abdominal pain, and after months of failed treatments, I found myself shipped off to a medical center in Boston where the physician who approached my bed looked older than father time.

"I have this pain in my belly," I said with anxiety.

The doctor swept medications from the top of my dresser into a wastebasket. "Shut up. I know what ails you. You have rebound acid-stomach from all these drugs."

While shocked by this reception, a decisive physician had rendered appropriate care and my symptoms disappeared.

When examining other physicians, slow and careful became my watchwords. Usually, I reserved two hours for their visits; and frequently, I offered small anecdotes to relax the atmosphere. I sympathized with these reluctant patients, who, after providing God-like health care, placed their naked bodies on cold examining tables— a disorienting experience, indeed.

During an insurance examination for an associate, I couldn't hear sounds in my stethoscope while measuring the blood pressure; and watching the meter became useless. I inflated the cuff a second time then slowly released the air. I heard nothing then checked the blood pressure using his other arm. The attempt failed. Not a sound reached my ears. Finally, I said, "Doctor, you don't have a blood pressure."

He twisted his face in anger. "Dummy, your stethoscope is on backwards. You can't hear a thing."

One day my secretary informed me about a special patient on my schedule.

"Who is it?" I asked.

"You're going to examine that busy cardiologist from the medical center. He has chest pain."

"I'm glad to see you," I told the physician who sat before my desk later in the day, "but certainly, others have evaluated your condition."

"The studies on my coronary arteries are normal, but I still have chest discomfort while breathing, low-grade fever and abnormal T-waves on several electrocardiograms."

"Your physical is completely normal," I informed him after finishing the examination. "I hope you were satisfied with my cardiac evaluation."

"You did fine. Just fine."

"Please, I need to perform one more maneuver. Turn over the table and rise up on your elbows and knees so I can listen under your heart while its thrust against your sternum. As you know, this position may reveal friction rubs of pericarditis."

Soon, my stethoscope detected the scratching sounds of pericardial inflammation.

Back at my desk, I explained that he needed serologic test to rule-out infectious causes of pericarditis; and several weeks later, at my request, a surgeon performed a biopsy of the physician's pericardial sac which grew Actinomycetes, an organism that spread to the physician's heart from an infected tooth. Before long, with antibiotic treatment, his symptoms disappeared.

As I sped toward the hospital on the empty blackened highway, I worried continuously about the task ahead. Despite bone-wrenching fatigue, my best efforts were required to examine this physician, and of course, I would need her complete confidence. In the darkness, I decided to perform slow world-class physical examination and resolved to do it each day on rounds.

On opening the door to the patient's room, a foul odor filled the air and I noticed her husband waiting anxiously beside the bed. At one a.m., I had arrived in casual clothing. A power statement? Hopefully, yes.

The skin felt hot, the neck seemed slightly stiff suggesting meningitis and a foul-smelling bandage covered the wound on the back; and I observed something else—cloudy fluid trickled down her spine. "Horror of horrors," I thought. "This physician has developed a wound infection, meningitis and also leaking spinal fluid. Surgery must have torn the dura, the covering of the spinal cord."

After informing the patient that this complication held a fatality rate of 80%, I explained that a terrible situation existed since the leak would continue in the presence of infection, and new organisms might enter the spinal canal while the dura remained open.

"I've had several patients with this difficult condition," I said, "and I've been forced to develop a new treatment—injection of powerful antibiotics directly into the spinal fluid. This approach has cured three patients, and shortly, this work will be published. I'll become famous if you survive."

She responded with laughter and her husband chuckled, too. "Go ahead. Let me make you famous."

Soon, the treatment started. Each day, I injected amikacin into the patient's spinal fluid and performed a head-to-toe physical examination. But several rocky moments developed when she demanded a Foley catheter for her bladder, which promptly became infected with yeast. Also, she requested a plastic catheter for neck veins to avoid needle punctures in the arms. I vetoed that idea since these devices frequently became contaminated with bacteria. Gradually, the patient's fever subsided, the meningitis cleared, and fluid stopped leaking from the back. Then, on the final day of hospitalization, I spoke with her about our relationship (she was a psychiatrist).

I sat on the edge of the bed and held her hand. "You demonstrated amazing courage while allowing experimental antibiotic treatment. Why did you remain in this local hospital when you could have flown to any medical center in the country—even the Mayo Clinic?"

"I never thought of using other doctors. You examined me completely each day that I lay ill."

"OK, Delilah. Tell it to me straight. Did you like it?"

"Yes, it's good but a bit scary. Your case is a prime example of how physicians frequently receive poor diagnosis and treatment. I liked this chapter."

"Delilah, I'm tired and need to go to bed. I'll stay awake until you play the music. What is it tonight?"

"Mozart's clarinet concerto."

Early the next morning, they cycled away from the house when the fog lifted, and now, Jerry found himself able to stay reasonably close to his leader. Before long, they reached the summit of the difficult hill, rested, and then enjoyed the view even though it was partially obscured by fog. They grabbed the drops of their handlebars, cocked their head upward and began the descent—a screaming exhilarating plunge into the valley below. Before long, they cycled on twisting country roads that led past green farms with cattle and barking dogs;

and about noon reached a trout pond. The sign read: Crosseyed Beaver. Fishing. Camping. Restaurant. Grist mill. Beside the sign, a poster held a picture of a beaver with eyes crossing toward the center of its nose.

They parked their bikes against a restaurant wall, climbed rickety steps and took a table beside a spinning waterwheel. The wheel held paddles about 12 inches apart and a column of water, from above, spilled onto the boards from a funnel that caused the wheel to turn. The paddles hit the stream below with a loud splash.

SPLASH! SPLASH! SPLASH!

The repetitive sounds of the turning water wheel and a fine mist enclosed the porch in a romantic atmosphere, and soon, a waitress approached the table. "Whole trout or fillet?"

"Two whole trout dinners, with French fries, hush puppies and coleslaw," Delilah replied. "Also, please bring two lemonades."

The waitress returned with lemonades, hush puppies and bowl of ground sesame sauce. "Dip the hush puppies into this."

"This is delicious," Jerry exclaimed.

SPLASH! SPLASH! SPLASH!

The water wheel continued its eternal duties—turning the grinding stone in the next building.

SPLASH! SPLASH! SPLASH!

Jerry extended his hand and covered Delilah's small fist. "I can't believe I'm here in this lovely place," he said as tears welled up in his eyes. "You're so beautiful and I'm so blessed." He began sobbing and uncontrollable crying that shook his whole body. "I'm so blessed. I'm so blessed."

SPLASH! SPLASH! SPLASH!

Delilah placed her other hand on top of Jerry's arm. "It's all right. I loved you from the moment I laid eyes on you. And rapture. Yes, I felt rapture when you touched my face. You are an aphrodisiac, a walking, talking, breathing aphrodisiac."

"I'm an aphrodisiac?"

"Yes, you are a handsome intelligent man who desperately loves me. Believe me, that's a wonderful turn on."

"Is something wrong?" the waitress asked as she brought two plates filled with food. "He's crying."

"He's fine. He's been through a lot. He just recovered from Alzheimer's disease. Now, he is trying to become an athlete."

"He doesn't look like a patient from a nursing home. He looks more like an athlete."

Jerry and Delilah dived into their food and quickly pulled sweet flesh off the trout's spine and munched on French fries and coleslaw.

SPLASH! SPLASH! SPLASH!

Soon, the waitress returned. "Do you want black bottom pie for dessert?"

"What type of food is that?"

"It's wonderful rum-flavored chocolate pudding with layers of custard and whipped cream."

"Bring two pies and two coffees, black, "Delilah instructed.

Soon, Jerry and Delilah mounted the saddles of their bikes and cycled back toward the city.

"Are we climbing that monster hill again?"

"Sure. We need to get ready for Europe."

Late in the afternoon, Delilah brought her favorite patient home where he collapsed on the sofa after showering. Soon, Delilah served angel hair spaghetti with a tangy red sauce.

"I need a day of rest tomorrow," Jerry insisted. "Also, I must pick up part of the manuscript from Melinda."

"We'll do sprint work in the morning."

"Why? We've had a huge day. My body is wasted."

"Look, muscles have two types of fibers—slow twitch and fast twitch. We need to develop both of these in order to climb. The fast twitch is used for speed and sprint work trains these tissues. We'll go to that isolated road by the lake and race back and forth as fast as possible. It's like the interval training used on the tracks by marathon runners. You'll enjoy it. It's exhilarating."

Jerry hung his head down looking at the carpet. "OK, Maybe I'll feel better in the morning. I can barely walk. Certainly, I won't have any energy for making love tonight."

Delilah smiled. "Jerry, you'll need to learn how to perform even with fatigue. It's part of your training."

"I need to perform tonight?"

"Yes."

"I can barely move."

"You don't need to do much. Just place your back on the bed and I'll do the rest."

"You will?"

"Yes."

"What music are you playing?"

"Bolero. Ravel's Bolero."

That sounds good to me. Put the disc in the machine. I'm going to bed."

Early in the morning, Jerry and Delilah placed their bikes in the van then drove to an isolated road beside a blue lake. They unloaded their machines, pulled on their helmets, then made themselves ready for the morning's drill.

"This road is one-mile long," Delilah declared. "Let's take two slow warm-up laps, return to the van then start a series of sprints to the end of the path, rest for a few seconds and race back. You must cycle as fast as possible. Push yourself. Push yourself hard and watch the computer on your handlebars to check the speed. We must build up our fast twitch fibers to climb long miles in Europe. Let's go."

They moved down the road at a deliberate pace and gazed at the lake as shafts of morning sunlight danced on the surface of the water. As they moved, the glitter seemed to follow them. At the end of the road, they turned their bikes around and slowly returned to the van.

"OK," Delilah yelled. "Let's go."

They sped down the road as if shot out of a cannon with Jerry grinning from ear to ear. "This is exciting," he yelled.

They dashed back and forth on the narrow strip, and at each end, stopped for a few seconds then sped off again but became progressively more exhausted.

"Let's try one more sprint," Delilah said. "Then, we'll slowly cycle back to cool down our muscles."

Finally, Jerry got the rest his muscles desperately needed and he gazed at the sparkling water while slowly returning to the van. A cool breeze caressed his face and he felt glued to the bike. "I feel part of this machine," he announced.

"That's good. You've become a cyclist."

They packed their bikes in the van, drove to Leon's office, picked up typed copies of Jerry's chapters then stopped at a small café for lunch.

"Melinda is editing and placing punctuation marks in the correct places," Jerry said with satisfaction. "I'm dictating three more chapters this afternoon.

"You're joking."

"No. I need to finish this book before leaving for Europe."

Later, Jerry sat on the sofa holding the dictating machine in one hand and notes in the other. Delilah sat beside him, pressing her back tightly against his.

"What's it about?"

"It concerns chess, learning to think, growing up as a small boy, heart attacks and caring for friends.

"That sounds interesting. Spit it out."

"Good morning, Melinda," Jerry said. "I'm dictating chapter 13. The title is CHECKMATE. Here it is."

While growing up as a small boy, my world seemed simple—learning ABC's, begging for long pants and listening to the Lone Ranger on the radio at night. In the darkness of my room, I let my imagination drift into dramatic western adventures, and at the end of the program, someone always asked: 'Who was that masked man?' Then, fading in the distance, I heard the most endearing call: 'Hi-Yo Silver, away.'

One Friday night, my life changed when an uncle from Russia joined us for the evening meal. Arriving with a box and board under his arm, he beckoned me beside the fireplace to learn the game of chess and spun my life forward in ways that I didn't understand.

At first, I learned the rules of the game, mimicked his moves on the board, and then gradually gave considerable thought to the placement of my pieces trying desperately not to lose my valuable army. Soon, my game became bolder, but as Fridays layered on Fridays, my uncle stood up each evening and announced, 'checkmate' when my trapped king had no space to move. This weekly ritual never concerned winning or losing—I had been invited beside the roaring flames to receive an uncle's love and lessons in thinking—gifts for a lifetime. Sometimes, amongst the warmth of the fire and delicious smells of orange pipe tobacco, my eyes closed for a few seconds, and then, an unknown force would lift me from the carpet and carry me away to a place of enchanting dreams.

Several years later, I lost interest in chess when my uncle's heart suddenly stopped, but my life rocketed forward with vitality while transferring thoughts into bold effective action. Many years later, after entering private practice, I noticed an older man playing chess in the corner of the room during an evening party. Saying not one word, I pulled a chair near the table, watching. Soon, the man said checkmate and his opponent rose to leave.

The man glanced at me, barely turning his head and said, "Do you play?"

"Years ago, as a small boy."

The pieces felt familiar, the moves seemed automatic and I initiated an attacking game without even thinking. But halfway through the match, Sid rose from the chair saying he intended to go home. "Won't you join me for chess one evening?"

"Sure. That will be interesting."

Soon, on a Friday after supper, I marched over to Sid's house to play chess and his wife led me to a living room with a fireplace in the corner; a pot of tea and cookies rested beside a table.

Using an antique chess set, I felt like Napoleon Bonaparte at Waterloo while moving the gorgeous pieces around the board. Suddenly, in the middle of the match, my mind transported me through an expanse of time, through the space of the earth, to an evening with my uncle when I was ten years old. Now, like that night long ago, I felt heat from the embers in the fireplace, smelt pipe tobacco and remembered my disappointment as my uncle advanced for another checkmate. But a chance to block checkmate and defeat appeared several moves ahead. If my uncle took my bishop with his knight, I could capture it with a pawn, which would shield my king causing a draw. Slowly, he advanced his knight, and my heart raced and my mouth felt dry. He pounced on my bishop, I grabbed his knight, and two moves later, my king slid behind the pawn blocking checkmate.

Sid said, "Your move."

"I know."

My uncle hesitated, inspected the board then rose from the table with his biggest smile.

"You've earned a draw," he said as my heart burst with joy.

"When are you going to move?" Sid asked with agitation.

"I think we have a draw. Let's do it again next Friday night."

Fridays drifted into Fridays, matches built on matches, and eventually, Sid became a patient making our relationship complex, indeed. Like my uncle, Sid always found strategies for winning and announced 'Checkmate' at the end of each evening. While I never purposefully lost a match, my weekly performance gave another human being a deep sense of satisfaction.

One day, I became less than enthusiastic about playing chess because rumors suggested that Sid and his wife might soon face divorce. But when Friday arrived, I shuffled off for my usual exercise in futility.

Sid's wife, however, didn't greet me at the door and tension filled in the air. On this night, my presence seemed most unwelcome. Unpleasant remarks filtered into the living room from the kitchen, and quickly, I tried ending the match. A pawn positioned badly. Snatched. A knight exposed. Gobbled up. A bishop moved to an endangered space. Picked off. My queen placed on the wrong side on the board. Gone. King in jeopardy. Then, he did it. He swooped down to my back row with his queen and said the word I longed to hear: Checkmate.

After a restless night, the telephone jarred me awake early in the morning, and I found Sid's voice quavering over the line.

"Will you come see me? I've had chest pains."

Barely breathing, nearly suffocating, this situation, similar to my uncle's illness seemed impossible, but quickly, I dressed and drove to Sid's house.

"Why didn't you call last night?"

"I didn't want to disturb you."

The pulse, slightly increased, had frequent extra beats; and the blood pressure, normal in the flat position, fell quite low when I placed him upright. Also, the second heart sound appeared widely split suggesting a right bundle branch block in the heart.

"This is a heart attack," I said while grabbing the telephone to call an ambulance. "I'll arrange for a cardiologist to care for you. I can't be your doctor anymore. We've spent too many evenings playing chess."

Later in that week, I stopped by the hospital to evaluate Sid's progress, and to my surprise, found him in the hall.

"I'm doing fine, only a minor heart attack."

Once again, during the following week, I visited Sid in the hospital. "Why are you still here? You look well."

"My doctor agreed to let me stay since I might fight with my wife at home."

Sid called me in my office later in the week.

"Can you come to the hospital before the end of the day?"

"Sure, do you want to bring a chess set?"

"No, just bring yourself."

Now, Sid looked in excellent condition after three weeks of hospitalization. He greeted me warmly.

"I'm leaving in the morning and need to tell you how much I've enjoyed our chess matches on Friday evenings. Those long hours at the board gave me a great deal of pleasure. But I'm going for good—disappearing at dawn so my wife can't find me. She caused this heart attack but won't get another chance to kill me. I've taken a lump-sum retirement and wired it overseas. She can have everything else—my house, my chess set, my car and my son. I want my life—that's all. In the morning, I'm embarking on a secret new existence."

"You sound like that character in Joseph Conrad's story, 'The Secret Sharer.' You know, the sailor who fled by diving off the ship near the Gulf of Siam."

"Yes. Yes. Yes. That's me. That's me. I'm just like that guy—swimming stroke by stroke toward a new life; and you're my secret sharer. Tomorrow, my wife will arrive to take me home but I'll have vanished from the face of the earth. Please keep my secret."

"All right. It's your life. Do you have medical clearance?"

"My doctor doesn't know. I'm fine."

"I'm sorry, Sid, but I need to go. Good luck and please stay well." I turned my head while walking toward the door. He smiled and waved. "Oh, by the way, checkmate."

"Delilah, did you like it?"

"It's charming and complicated. What's next?"

"It's about the value of plowing through medical articles in the library. Physicians must keep current with the new literature to offer patients the latest treatments. Here it is."

"Hello, Melinda. It's Jerry again. I'm dictating chapter 14. The title is, THE TABLE. I hope you like it."

On Wednesday afternoons, wonderful Wednesdays, the library in the medical center became my destination; and here, among the silent book-lined shelves, I found peace, solitude and knowledge.

Crowding the entrance to the facility, a long thin table precariously gripped new medical journals that lay scattered, twisted and jumbled all about. If this scene had been a groaning board filled with food, it would have been unappetizing, indeed. But here, the table held nourishments for the mind. Early each morning, librarians added new publications, and by the end of the week, the table became heavy with the articles about the latest medical advances. But then, on Friday afternoons, they swept it clean allowing the process to begin anew on Monday mornings.

After entering the library, I snatched journals from one end of the table, moved forward, collected anything of interest, and then, with prizes in hand, and retreated to a comfortable chair in the corner of the room.

One afternoon, I fielded a magazine of general biology—not a clinical publication. Here, an article described a treatment for aspergillosis, a fungal infection that becomes lethal after entering the

104

blood or brain. In this study, mice survived when researchers added rifampin to the standard antifungal drugs. "This is interesting," I thought while copying the article for my files. The following week, a neurosurgeon's call disturbed my tranquility in the library.

"Will you look at a specimen?" he asked over the telephone. "I found a patient's frontal lobe rock-hard after performing a craniotomy. It might be an infection!"

In the hospital's laboratory, a scraping from the patient's brain had been floated on a glass slide, and under the lens of the microscope, a fungus appeared with the characteristic side chains of Aspergillus species. "This patient must have aspergillosis," I thought while grabbing the telephone to call the surgeon. "Your patient has a fatal fungal infection of the brain."

"See the patient anyway," he replied in an angry voice.

A 35-year-old businessman had developed a left maxillary sinusitis that broke upward through the orbital bone then infected his brain. After reviewing the CT scan, a mass appeared in the frontal lobe with tentacles that extended toward the center of the head. The patient's father waited outside the patient's hospital room.

"What are his chances, Doc?"

"I'm sorry. His prospects are zero. This fungus has spread deep into the brain and he'll die when it strikes a major artery."

"Will you tell him? I'm not sure he can take those words."

"Yes. I must speak frankly to your son in order to start some type of treatment."

I opened the door and found the patient awake even though surgery had been performed earlier in the day.

His wife waited beside the bed, holding his hand.

"My doctor said I have a fungal infection," he muttered. "Give it to me straight—what are my chances?"

"I am very sorry. This fungus has spread deep into the center of your brain. Your chances are zero."

"I've done many shady business deals. God has passed judgment."

"With your permission, I would like to try a new treatment that has been found effective for mice but it hasn't been used in humans. I just read the article."

"What could be worse than zero. I"ll try anything. Go ahead—make me a test mouse."

"OK, I'll treat you with the standard antifungal medications but add a medicine used for the treatment of tuberculosis—rifampin. When researchers used this drug to treat aspergillus infections in mice, the little critters survived. On the positive side, I am glad to tell you that rifampin easily enters brain tissue and high levels of this medication should reach your infection. I'll start this new treatment at once. Does your wife agree?"

"Yes," she mumbled.

"I must mention that one medication, amphotericin B, will damage your kidneys but they will recover if your survive."

One week later, the patient's CT scan revealed that the fungal prongs no longer extended outward from the frontal lobe, and after an additional week of treatment, the fungal mass appeared smaller.

"Your chances have improved today," I told the patient with a smile. "We're making medical history. You'll make me famous."

"Great. I want to make you famous."

After six weeks of treatment, a CT scan of the brain appeared completely normal.

"Now there is real hope," I informed the patient over the telephone. "It's time to stop treatment. But I'll need to repeat your CT scan next month. Come to my office after the procedure since additional drugs might be required if there are any signs of relapse."

The patient called my office several weeks later after his scan.

"Your infection has vanished," I said. "Come anyway, so we can plan additional tests later in the year.

Tears flowed down the patient's cheeks as he came through my office corridor. .

"Mr. Zero has survived. Mr. Zero has survived," he cried. "I've led a selfish life but God has given me another chance. Now, I'll work only for charity and other good causes. I'll not forsake my God, ruler of the Universe."

The wife sat in front of my desk and spoke in a hushed voice: "Doctor, how did you pull this off? This is a real miracle."

I smiled and patted her hand. "The medical library has a table. It's a long messy table filled with journals."

"Well, Delilah. Was it good?"

"Sure. Sure. It's fine. You performed a miracle for that patient. Did he ever learn how you did it?"

"Not really. He knew I found the article but he didn't understand my long determination to keep abreast of the medical literature. You know, over the years, I never saw another practicing physician in that medical library. By the way, I have one more chapter this afternoon."

"What's it about?"

"It concerns the hospitalization of sick patients who enter the emergency room for care. But its more than that. Something miraculous happened to me during my last night on call. I received a gift—a blessed gift."

"From where?"

"I don't know. Someone watched over me that evening and cared for me. Here we go."

"Hello, Melinda. It's Jerry again with chapter 15. It's title is, THE LAST NIGHT CALL."

Day and night, internists stand-by, on call, to hospitalize seriously ill medical patients from emergency rooms but are released from this arduous obligation after reaching 50 years of age. This duty, lasting 24 hours, is described as 'night call' since the action usually begins after sundown.

A 50th birthday and my last night call arrived simultaneously, but this celestial conjunction of events appeared ill-timed since I planned a desperately needed vacation in just three days. Worrying continuously, I thought it might be impossible to find doctors to cover my practice if I hospitalized patients during my last service to the community. "Somehow," I thought, "I had be on a plane to California in just 72 hours."

The ticking clock of night call started gently but good fortune vanished at nine p.m.

"I have an alcoholic patient with seizures," the emergency room physician informed me. "He needs hospitalization."

Since the patient's studies revealed low blood glucose and a normal brain scan, I felt confident that alcohol caused the man's seizures. But while finishing the examination, the emergency room physician tapped me on the shoulder. "Doctor, I have a narcotic addict who is vomiting blood."

"Horror of horrors," I thought, "Another critically ill patient needs care."

Working fast, I secured the services of a gastroenterologist who stopped the patient's bleeding, but now, two seriously ill individuals rested under my wing. Suddenly, a hysterical old patient called and demanded the immediate transfer of her records, which forced me to the copying machine for an hour. Exhausted, I retreated to my office, closed my eyes in a chair, and while drifting into a twilight zone between drowsiness and sleep, the ringing telephone jolted me awake.

"I have a patient with pneumonia," the voice announced. "He just buried his wife."

Nearly paralyzed, operating on one cylinder, I entered a small cubicle in the emergency room at three a.m.

"How are you feeling, Mr. Jones?"

"He's sick," a daughter muttered.

"Are you coughing?"

"He just lost his wife," remarked another daughter.

"Please. I need to speak with the patient."

"We're his daughters."

"OK. OK," I said. "Just let me finish."

The physical examination confirmed the diagnosis of pneumonia and I wrote hospital orders that included intravenous antibiotics and nasal oxygen. "Now," I thought, "I've suffered a complete calamity—three seriously ill patients are on my service with only two days before departure." I called the emergency room at five a.m.

"Do you have other patients that might need hospitalization?"

"No. All is quiet."

"Thank God. Thank God."

Before going home, I decided to check the widower with pneumonia, and on opening the door to the patient's room, noticed that the oxygen catheter had fallen from his nose. Silently, I lifted the life-giving tube of air into his nostrils. "Now," I thought, "it is time for me to rest."

The following afternoon, I awoke with anxiety and foreboding as the digital clock blinked three p.m. "For sure," I thought, "I won't find doctors who will care for three sick patients." Discouraged and depressed, I dressed then raced back to the hospital where fatigue drenched my body like an Indian monsoon. I started rounds on the hospital's top floor.

"How is the man with seizures?" I asked the nurse. "Any more episodes?"

"I don't believe you need to worry about epilepsy, doctor. We found his room empty this morning."

"Gone?"

"Gone," she echoed. "He must have had a powerful thirst."

"Good," I thought. "One gone but two sick patients remained. I changed floors by walking down two flights of stairs.

"How is the bleeding narcotic addict?" I questioned the nurse.

"I'm not really sure. Only the patient knows that answer."

"OK. Let's examine her together."

"That won't be necessary. She disappeared during the night— probably needed another fix."

"Gone?"

"Gone," she echoed.

Now, my night call disaster held only a widower with pnenmonia as my name boomed over the hospital's loudspeaker.

"You have a call," the nurse said.

"This is Mr. Jones' daughter," the voice said over the telephone. "You examined my father last night."

"Yes, I remember. I'm coming to see him in a few minutes."

"Not on you life. You're fired!"

"Fired?"

"Yes, fired."

"I don't understand."

"My veterinarian had more feeling for my dog last week than you had for my dad in the emergency room. The chief-of-staff will take over his case."

"Miss," I said with measured anger, "I checked your father before leaving the hospital. He lost his oxygen during the night and I placed the tube of air back into his nose. I don't believe any other doctor would have been there at five a.m."

Shocked, I sat in the nurses' station holding my head in my hands.

"The master puppeteer pulled strings last night—just for me," I thought. "Now, I'll enjoy a long rest in California. Yes, I've worked hard helping others. Someone has been keeping score."

"Jerry, you're a good person. The master puppeteer watched over you during that last night on call. You needed to survive as much as patients needed care. I liked the story. Let's go out to dinner. I know a great Chinese restaurant."

Later, that evening, Jerry and Delilah entered a hiking shop to buy equipment for their trip. Delilah put her arm around Jerry's shoulder.

"Two backpacks will serve as our bags and we'll need to buy bright red nylon parkas to ward off the rain. We'll tie them under the handlebars. Also, we'll need to buy light weight rain pants and then stow them in our saddle bags."

"I'm getting excited," Jerry said effusively. "I can't wait to board that airplane for Europe."

Delilah frowned and looked pensive. "I want you to buy hiking boots for this trip since we might take a side trip to Innsbrook. We should have spectacular scenery during high altitude walks and the old city offers romantic candlelight dinners in the streets. Look, this Danner Lite boot is waterproof and its heal is constructed with a unique wedge that lifts the foot during climbing."

Immediately, Jerry fitted his feet into a Danner boot size 10 ½ EE and it felt wonderful. "I'll wear these boots on the plane to Prague."

Later that evening, Jerry sat on the sofa watching television and held Delilah's hand.

"I plan to provide for your in the future. I'll promote my book on a national tour and apply to medical schools to teach physical diagnosis. We'll pick a city that will allow plenty of recreational activities."

"Are you proposing marriage?"

"Maybe. Let's work on it when we return from Europe."

Delilah became restless. "Jerry, you must stop planning your future and must suspend working on your book. The purpose of this European adventure is to free our souls of all earthly concerns. For a little while, let's step off the world and renew ourselves. We can't free our spirits if you're searching for a publisher and applying to medical schools. I need our help with the maps and the selection of hotels."

"I see. You want me to begin concentrating on this trip immediately?"

"Yes."

"OK, I'll give our adventure my undivided attention. I need, however, to finish the last few chapters of the book and the epilogue. Also, I need to send a letter to my literary agent. I'll dictate this piece now. OK?"

"Good evening, Melinda. I'm not able to receive the manuscript until after my return from Europe. I would, however, like you to proofread two chapters (number one, A SECRET CONSULTATION and number three, THE MOST BEAUTIFUL GIRL. Please send copies to my literary agent Mr. Robert Silverstone 1100 Fifth Avenue, N.Y. N.Y. Please look up the zip code. Please mail these materials with the following letter: Dear Bob.

I will be grateful if you will try to find a publisher for my book entitled, 'THE ROMANCE OF BEDSIDE DIAGNOSIS. I have enclosed two sample chapters. The full manuscript will be ready for review after my return from Europe. Unfortunately, I will not be available for conferences during this trip but will accept any reasonable deal. My attorney, Mr. Leon Rittenbaum, can sign, if necessary, any document during my absence. Melinda, please add Leon's address."

"Also," Jerry continued, "I am enclosing a brief book proposal as follows: This narrative concerns the adventure and triumph of bedside diagnosis as physicians weave their magic through the fabric of human drama. This work, the first to sweep readers into the art of bedside medicine, will inspire and entertain as the author plies his craft among colorful individuals, friends and colleagues. The audience for this book includes 800,000 physicians, 7 million ancillary medical personnel, 76,000 medical students and the lay public as well. Markets include 125 bookstores attached to medical schools and thousands of doctors who attend monthly medical meetings."

Bob, I appreciate your efforts on my behalf. I'll call you on my return.

Best Regards. Jerome Stern, M.D."

"That's it, Melinda. Good night."

"Delilah, I'll dictate the final chapters and the epilogue in the morning while you're out shopping. Then, I'll free my mind for this journey. What music are you playing tonight?"

"John Denver's songs."

"I like John Denver's music. He sings about the soul. He sings about love. Please, place the disc in the machine and let's go to bed."

The following week, Leon represented Jerry at a hearing, and immediately, the court rescinded his legal confinement to Heavenly Manor. Also, Jerry decided to continue twice daily exercises at the hospital's center for physical therapy. "I'm progressing faster with cross training equipment," he told Delilah. "I'll be ready for our trip— body and soul."

Chapter Ten

CYCLING PRAGUE TO VIENNA

The day before their flight to Prague, Jerry and Delilah carefully placed their bikes in large cardboard boxes then filled the extra space with thick foam to prevent damage by transport workers.

"I'm worried about the weather in Eastern Europe," Jerry declared. "The rains are continuing and many rivers are overflowing their banks."

"Jerry, don't worry, we'll sit tight in Prague until the weather clears. There are interesting things to see in this famous capital. It's neither pleasant nor safe to cycle into a monsoon."

The next day, they drove their van to Washington D.C., left it with a friend, then rode a taxi to Dulles International airport for their flight to Prague via Vienna. Soon, they found themselves lifting off for their soul-saving adventure.

Delilah snuggled close to Jerry. "I'm feeling better already."

Jerry seemed agitated. "Today, the rains are worse in Eastern Europe."

Delilah squeezed his hand. "Don't worry. We'll overcome all difficulties in the weeks ahead. This is an adventure."

In the morning, after landing in Vienna, Jerry and Delilah transferred to a small shuttle airplane that rose into black skies, and before long, the aircraft descended toward Prague but repeatedly circled the airport as wind and rain buffeted their approach.

Jerry held the seat tightly with both hands. "That was a difficult landing. I hope the rest of the trip is smoother."

In the baggage area, Jerry and Delilah extracted their bikes, discarded the cardboard boxes, pulled backpacks on their shoulders then wheeled their machines outside the airport searching for a taxi as a cold wind-driven rain slashed their faces.

An elderly driver, sitting in a large cab, waved to them, and directly, he loaded their bikes then began a slow drive toward the center of Prague.

"My God," Delilah declared, "the rivers are over their banks, the streets are flooded and signs are under water, too.'

"This is the 100-year flood," the driver said with a thick accent. "The police have closed the famous Charles Bridge."

Jerry frowned. "This is terrible. Look, the bike paths are gone."

Soon, the taxi passed over a high bridge, turned left then arrived at the Olsanka hotel.

"This place used to be the headquarters of the communist party," the driver said. "The rooms and food are just fair but they have live music in the lounge every night."

"We'll need special services."

"Yes. Yes. Where you go?"

"In several days, we need to be dropped off outside the city for two hours to test our bikes. Can you do that and pick us up again?"

"Yes. Yes. No problem."

"OK," Delilah said. "I'll call you. Also, in three or four days, we'll need our backpacks dropped off at a hotel 100 kilometers to the south."

"Yes. Yes. I give good price."

"Give me your card and I'll call you soon."

Jerry and Delilah collapsed in bed to recover from their long flight then awoke in the late afternoon. They pulled on their rain parkas hoping for a stroll, but the bulletin board in the lobby revealed discouraging notices. "All museums closed. Prague castle closed. Jewish quarter closed. All rivers rising."

"What is left to see in Prague?" Delilah asked a manager of the hotel.

"You can walk in city and look at beautiful buildings. Also, a famous glass blowing factory is just north of the city. The number 15 bus will take you there."

Jerry and Delilah tried walking outside the hotel but a heavy rain forced them back.

"Let's rest, eat and listen to music in the lounge," Delilah suggested. "Tomorrow, we'll walk in the city then visit the glass blowing factory in the afternoon."

"That sounds good to me."

After dinner, Jerry and Delilah retreated to the lounge where a duo played soft romantic music with a violin and cello. Delilah draped her arms around Jerry's neck, he clasped his hands together behind the small of her back and they barely moved while swaying back and forth on the dance floor.

"I love you," she murmured. "I'll never let you go."

Sunny skies greeted Jerry and Delilah in the morning as they stepped onto a number 12 for the ride to the old city. They walked to the Jewish quarter but found police standing in front of barricades. Beyond, water filled the street and sand bags guarded the front doors of most houses. They felt themselves in another world while walking among old buildings topped by high spires, but sand bags blocked the doors of all museums. Soon, they walked to Wencelas square, the site of revolutionary activities. Delilah moved her arm in all directions. "This is where history evolved."

"Let's eat lunch and visit the glass blowing factory," Jerry suggested. "I want to buy a gift for Melinda."

They enjoyed beef Stroganoff in a small café then boarded a bus for the glass blowing factory, where on a tour, the guide described all the old techniques. After buying an etched glass bowl, they returned to the hotel to organize their clothes for the morning's test ride of their bikes.

"Our bicycles must be in perfect condition before we head south toward Vienna," Delilah declared.

The next day, clear skies greeted Jerry and Delilah as they waited outside the hotel for the taxi.

"Are waters still rising in the rivers?" Jerry asked the driver.

"Yes. North rivers flood Prague. Police close more bridges."

They snaked their way through traffic, and then, just after entering the bridge, police stopped the car. The driver rolled down the window and spoke heatedly with the man. Finally he said, "They close this bridge. No can come back this way. They close all bridges in Prague except one on the other side of the city. I drive 80 kilometers back to hotel. You're stay in taxi? Yes?"

"No," Delilah said emphatically. "We'll cycle back to Prague."

"Eighty kilometers is a 50 mile warm-up ride," Jerry said with rising anxiety.

"You bike downtown Prague and old city?" the driver asked.

"Yes. It will be an adventure. A thrill. We'll cycle into one of Europe's most beautiful cities. Let's do it."

Jerry and Delilah left the taxi and began cycling beside green landscapes then stopped to plan their day-long ride to Prague. Periodically, they adjusted of their seats and handlebars, and eventually, riding close together, reached a smooth rhythm. "This is wonderful," Jerry yelled.

About noon, they found a cosy café in a small village and enjoyed veal and noodles.

"No beer," Delilah instructed. "We'll need all our energy to finish this day."

Late in the afternoon, they crested a long hill, stopped at the summit and gazed down at hundreds of colorful spires that rose from the city of Prague. They grabbed the drops of their handlebars, clicked shoes into pedals and pushed off, downhill. Faster and faster, power through the curves, power in their legs, they rapidly descended as the gorgeous capital swept upward before their eyes. Before long, they entered downtown in the middle of heavy traffic.

"Stay close to me," Delilah yelled. "Ride close to the curb."

After awhile, they found themselves in the old city and gazed fondly at the medieval structures. "I'm weak," Jerry yelled. "My muscles are out of fuel."

Delilah placed Jerry flat on a bench and offered power bars and liquids. "We'll start looking an open bridge when you feel better."

In a while, they cycled onward searching for the bridge but found span after span barricaded and guarded by police.

"Bridge? Bridge?" Delilah shouted.

Police pointed straight ahead, and finally, around a bend in the road, Delilah spotted the tall structure that would take them across the river to their hotel. Jerry heard a loud hiss from his front tire.

"Flat. Flat," he yelled.

Delilah pedaled back to him and examined the situation.

"There is still some air left in the tire. You can make it back to the hotel."

Slowly, they moved off the bridge as Jerry labored with the soft tire. "I'm finished. I can't go on."

"OK. Stay here. I'll come back for you with a taxi."

Before long, Delilah rescued Jerry, brought him to the hotel, and in their room, helped him strip off his clothes.

"Shower and rest," she instructed. "We'll have a late dinner then dance in the lounge."

Later, after a reasonable meal, they walked into the lounge and began enjoying the music. On the dance floor, they swayed back and forth holding each other for dear life.

Jerry whispered in Delilah's ear. "You've rescued me a second time."

"You did fine. You would have made it back to the hotel if your tire remained full of air."

In the morning, the hotel's management offered good news: "The Ultava River crested during the night, water levels have receded and police have reopened some bridges.

"Tomorrow," Delilah declared, "we're leaving Prague, cycling toward Cesky Krumlov, a 15th century medieval town. It's 200 kilometers directly to the south. We'll stay in a charming hotel—an old restored Jesuit monastery."

"We can't cycle 200 kilometers in a single day."

"We'll break up the trip and sleep overnight in Tabor—a 100 kilometer ride. Today, let's rest, study maps and get organized for our departure. So far, our journey has had a spectacular beginning. I'll never forget our downhill plunge into Prague."

"I can use the rest. I'm still tired from yesterday's grand adventure."

The following day, the taxi driver dropped Jerry and Delilah at the edge of Prague then headed south with their backpacks. While cycling into flat terrain they felt exhilaration, and in the sunshine, using a leisurely pace, arrived in Tabor in the afternoon full of energy. Relieved to find their packs in the hotel, they showered, rested then enjoyed dinner in room with tapestry-covered walls. Most depicted scenes of monks working in the fields. "Tomorrow," Delilah declared, "we're cycling to Cesky Krumlov, a real Bohemian treasure. As we approach this quaint town from the road, we'll be transported back into the 15th century."

Jerry and Delilah enjoyed their ride to Cesky Krumlov and found it nestled into a huge S bend of the Ultava River, but were shocked to see watermarks that reached above the first floor windows of many buildings. Krumlov Castle, colored in pink, guarded over the town from above.

The inhabitants of this town must have fled during the flood," Jerry suggested.

On entering their hotel, they found their rooms with a huge window overlooking the beautiful plaza, and that evening, enjoyed a candlelight dinner, held hands and reminisced about their smooth ride.

"I'm shocked to my roots by this exciting exotic adventure," Jerry declared.

"The best is yet to come. Let's finish our meal then enjoy chamber music in the city theater."

Soon, they walked into the dimly lit public square, gazed at the brightly illuminated Krumlov castle above and found seats in an indoor arena with a small stage in the center of a bowel. Soon, a string quartet entered then caressed them with the delicate sounds of a Shubert concerto; and afterwards, they sat on a bench in the square planning the next day's journey.

"We'll face extensive climbing in the morning," Delilah said. "The border between the Czech Republic and Austria sits on a high plateau. I think we'll enjoy a spectacular plunge into Austria, but to get there, our muscles need to perform. Linz, an industrial town, is our next destination. It's not too far."

"Don't worry. I'm getting stronger with each passing day."

In the morning, clear skies greeted Jerry and Delilah, but almost immediately, the road angled steeply upward.

"Take it easy," Delilah yelled. "It's going to be tough cycling."

Several hours later, Jerry and Delilah spotted the guard station at the Czech border then stood in line with cars and trucks. They received smiles from agents in the passport control, and then, were passed over to the Austrian border station. From there, they rode on flat terrain for a short distance then noticed a steep descent. Far below, the green landscape of Austria unfolded before their eyes.

"Put on your windbreaker," Delilah instructed. "This will be a long cold ride into Austria."

They grabbed the drops of their handlebars, cocked their heads upward, clicked shoes into pedals and slowly moved their bikes downhill. Faster and faster, sweeping through the curves, they thrust themselves downward as green vineyards and lush farmland rose to meet them. Delilah's long auburn hair billowed out beneath her helmet.

"Oh my God," Jerry yelled. "Yahoo! Yahoo!"

Steep downhill roads greeted Jerry and Delilah much of the day, but in the late afternoon, after reaching the outskirts of Linz, and much searching, they found the old section of town where beautiful hotels and colorful outdoor restaurants encircled a large plaza. They pushed their bikes into the elevator of the hotel, felt joy to see their packs in the room, showered, rested then ate a delicious dinner outdoors while planning the next day's journey. "We're riding to Durnstein, a gorgeous old village above the Danube," Delilah said. "It sits on a ridge among the vineyards."

The following morning, good weather prevailed as they entered bike paths beside the Danube river. But recent floods deposited layers of mud on the pavement, and periodically, they stopped in small villages to wash the debris off their shoes and pedals.

"I almost fell," Jerry declared. "I couldn't get my shoe out of the dirty cleat.

Suddenly, a woman in a small car began gesturing to them and honking. Alarmed, Delilah decided to follow her on the main road, and soon, on reaching a store, a man who spoke English explained the reason for the encounter.

"Bike path three feet under water," he said. "You must stay on the main highway."

Jerry and Delilah continued their ride, and before long, reached Mauthausen with its austere Nazi labor camp sitting high on a hill. After some discussion, they decided not to enter their solemn museum of death since it might dampen their spirits for the entire day.

"Look at that small road in the vineyards above us," Delilah declared. "Let's ride up there."

They cycled on this small path, stopped to taste grapes, and before long, reached their hotel on the outskirts of Durnstein. At dinner, Delilah released her plans for the following day. "We'll cycle north of Vienna, head east then stop at a beautiful spa, Bad Vslava. It will be a two night stay."

"Why two nights?"

"We'll soak our bodies in warm sulfur baths tomorrow afternoon, and the following day, enjoy a ride to Bratislava, the capital of Slovakia.

"That sounds interesting but a long, long day."

"Yes, but it will be worth the effort. A luxurious spa and another European capital awaits us."

The next day, as Jerry and Delilah cycled away from the hotel, they entered the village of Durnstein, medieval and colorful. They moved slowly through the city then continued cycling through Austria circling north and east of Vienna. Finally, in late afternoon, near sunset, they reached the spa town of Bad Vslav, entered the hotel, parked their bikes, showered, rested, then pulled on thick white robes for the walk to the sulfur pools.

"Oh. Oh!" Jerry exclaimed. "This feels wonderful. This hot sulfur water is leaching the pain from my legs and neck. It's wonderful. It's wonderful. I'm in heaven."

Soon, the heat and dehydration forced Jerry and Delilah out of the pool, and quickly, they showered and went to dinner, totally famished. "What a day," Jerry exclaimed. "Our cups runneth over."

"Tomorrow, we'll leave early, cycle to Bratislava, enjoy a leisurely lunch, view the city then ride back to the spa for another warm soak in the sulfur pool."

"Great! Great! We don't deserve such joy."

Once again, clear skies greeted Jerry and Delilah as they cycled away from the spa in the direction of the capital of Slovaka. After checking themselves through both passport control areas, they rode a few miles then entered the city.

"Here, time stands still," Jerry said while viewing the dilapidated buildings and old trolleys in Bratislava. In the distance, they heard a choir of singing gut-wrenching ancient melodies, and promptly, they rode into a plaza where a large group, dressed in costumes, stood before an ornate church. Jerry and Delilah rested beside their bikes and listened in awe, transported back in time. Then, with a deliberate pace, they rode beside old buildings, soaked up the atmosphere, then rested in an attractive outdoor restaurant.

Against their better judgment, they began enjoying delicious Pilsner beer before a lunch that included pasta, vegetables, coffee and dessert.

"Drink extra coffee," Delilah instructed. "We can't cycle back to the spa in a tipsy condition."

They saddled up, rode to the border station, and then, Austrian guards directed them to paved bike paths, a short distance away. Twin poles, about two feet apart, prevented motor vehicles from entering the route reserved for cyclists.

Delilah rode directly between the posts, but Jerry struck his elbow on the one of the stakes and tumbled to the ground. "I'm down," he yelled. "I'm down and bleeding."

Delilah turned around, helped Jerry off the ground, cleaned the wound with an alcohol sponge then applied a band-aid. "This doesn't need stitches but you won't be able to soak tonight in the sulfur pools."

The next day, on a narrow paved path beside the Danube river, Jerry and Delilah began a slow meandering ride toward Vienna. They noticed barges plowing through the muddy tributary but passenger boats didn't appear.

"Be careful," Delilah yelled. "The rains and floods have broken up the pavement."

About noon, they pulled off the bike path to enjoy lunch in a small village, and as usual, Delilah ordered pasta. Soon, they resumed their journey. "Let's pick up the pace," Delilah suggested. "I'd like to reach the hotel by the middle of the afternoon."

Delilah took the lead, they pedaled as hard as possible toward the romantic city of Vienna, and watched the Danube, muddy and filled with floating debris. Soon, they reached the outskirts of the city but felt shocked on entering an industrial zone.

"This is ugly," Jerry declared. "Where is beautiful Vienna?"

"It's in the old city, not here."

Delilah stopped for instruction to the center of town, became confused, and soon, large trucks surrounded both bikes.

"This is not safe. Let's find a taxi to take us in."

Dropped off at their hotel, they showered, rested, slept then pulled on their outfits for dinner. Delilah approached the clerk in the lobby asking for advice.

"We want a romantic restaurant with good food."

"Try the Blue Duck. It's expensive, but the food is good. The place has a dance floor, and a woman entertains patrons with a zither."

"A zither? That sounds wonderful."

Arm in arm, Jerry and Delilah walked several blocks north of the hotel in the old city, found the restaurant, descended a small staircase and heard the zither releasing the delicate sounds of the Third Man Theme. A tall woman sat before a table with a flat instrument, plucking the strings. They took a small table beside the dance floor and ordered white wine as sweet harp-like sounds of the zither surrounded them with magic.

Delilah smiled and whispered. "Here is the romance of Vienna."

"Yes. Yes, indeed."

They enjoyed their meal, finished it with gusto then stepped onto the dance floor as the musician played old songs—Begin the Begin, As Time Goes By, The White Cliff of Dover, and Strangers in the Night.

Delilah circled her arms around Jerry's neck. "Jerry, I've safely brought you to Vienna. I'll never let you go."

"Yes. Yes. I'm in heaven."

The musician played Edith Piaf's favorite song, "La vie en rose," and now, softly sang the melody.

> *Quand il me prend dans ses bras*
> *Il me parle tout bas*
> *Je vois la vie en rose*
> *Il me dit des mots d'amour.*

Transported back in time, Jerry and Delilah swayed back and forth on the dance floor as the entire audience joined a sing-along.

> *Quand il me prend dans ses bras*
> *Il me parle tout bas*
> *Je vois la vie en rose*
> *Il me dit des mot d'amour.*

They stepped back to their table where Delilah kissed Jerry on the cheek. "That was wonderful. Tomorrow, we'll explore Vienna on foot. Let's stroll in the Grand Ring, visit monuments and beautiful gardens, listen to street music, enjoy lunch in an outdoor café and spend time in the museums. We'll fill our souls with the splendor of this city."

"I need to visit the home of Sigmund Freud. I'd like to see that couch where he invented psychoanalysis. I called the tourist bureau and they said if one rings the bell, you will be invited upstairs like an expected guest. Let's do it."

"Sure. But we'll need to find boxes for our bikes since our flight to Marseilles leaves the day after tomorrow."

"We are leaving for France? I thought you were considering hiking in Innsbruck."

"No. We must reach Provence before large tour buses flood the area. We'll hike in Innsbruck another day."

The next evening, after a long day of walking in Vienna, Jerry and Delilah packed their bikes, organized their packs and arranged for transport to the airport. And the following morning, their aircraft lifted off, circled, and allowed views of beautiful Vienna far below.

Jerry's thought raced over the past week's adventure, again and again. "You've blessed me with an incredible experience. Why me?"

Delilah squeezed his hand and pulled it into her lap. "I love you. I love you."

Chapter Eleven

THE SOUTH OF FRANCE

Jerry and Delilah landed in Marseille's small airport, retrieved their backpacks but searched in vain for their bicycles. Finally, Delilah approached the baggage claims department, presented stubs from their tickets, and promptly, the clerk lifted the receiver from a telephone, spoke a few words over the line, then pointed his hand toward to the rear of the building. "You go big doors," he said. "Big doors."

Soon, Jerry and Delilah found a wall with large sliding panels, and shortly, it opened and revealed two Frenchmen holding large cardboard boxes. Smiling, they walked forward. "Tour de France?" one man asked.

"No. No. No," Delilah yelled. "Biking holiday. Biking holiday." She grabbed their hands and shook them with profound gratitude.

Jerry grabbed a rolling cart for the boxes and moved them to a wall holding a bank of telephones. Delilah called Renalt Rental Car Agency, and before long, they loaded gear in a large van, then drove to the Best Western hotel where the manager graciously agreed to hold their empty boxes until their return from their French adventure.

Jerry strapped the bikes to the rear walls of the van using safety belts then drove toward Aix-en-Provence, 14 kilometers to the north. "I'm in a delicious state of euphoria," he said. "Imagine, we'll soon explore another romantic European city. I'm pinching myself. First, we enjoyed a fantastic journey between Prague and Vienna, and now, here we are—in the fabled south of France."

"I've found a nice B and B just north of the city. We'll explore 'Aix' in the morning."

Shortly, the van entered heavy traffic on a long boulevard that circled inside Aix en Provence and Jerry became excited. "Wow! This is a big town. Where is the old city?"

"It's deep in the interior. Tomorrow, We'll patrol its interesting streets. Watch for a sign to Coventry. We'll need to turn then head north for a few miles."

In a while, Jerry and Delilah found the B and B, a house remodeled to receive guests. The owner, a retired engineer, greeted them warmly, stored their bikes in his garage then recommended a restaurant with for dinner.

The next morning, Jerry and Delilah shivered on entering their van—the gauge in the mirror read five degrees.

"Put on the heat," Delilah instructed. "It's about 40 degrees Farenheit."

They drove to the old city, found a sport shop, bought hats, gloves and liner sweaters then entered a throng of people parading through the streets. The crowd moved as a single thing and no one seemed to be shopping. Occasionally, they entered art, pottery, cloth and flower shops to inspect the wares.

By and by, Jerry and Delilah entered a large square converted into a gigantic outdoor market where vendors sold vegetables, olive oil, soaps, meats, art and pottery. Here, hundreds of people eagerly filled shopping bags; and many sat in outdoor restaurants sipping coffee or drinking beer. Music from an accordion filled the air. Delilah went from stall to stall, laughing. "This is fun."

After inspecting the market, they entered a narrow alley that led to the most beautiful street in Aix-en-Provence—the Coors Mirabeau. Plane trees, with sculpted tops and upturned branches, soared 80 to 100 feet in the air, and outdoor cafes, elegant hotels, fountains and statues lined each side of the avenue.

Delilah beamed from ear to ear. "This is gorgeous. In the summer, those branches must unite from tree to tree and form an awning over the entire street. Let's get some coffee."

Jerry frowned and became agitated. "It's getting colder. Those black clouds are going to dump rain on us in a few minutes."

Almost immediately, a cold wind-driven rain laced the Coors

Mirabeau and Jerry and Delilah, holding hands, raced to a small Italian restaurant they had spotted earlier in the morning. Delilah looked pensive and said little during lunch.

"We need to change plans. We can't enjoy 'Aix' in these conditions. Let's pick up our gear then drive north. I think we can reach the Luberon Valley before dark."

"Anything of interest along the way?"

"Yes. We'll stop at the artist village of Lourmarin."

Without delay, they loaded their van, drove northward on a winding narrow road in heavy rain, and about an hour later, reached Lourmarin and parked their van beside an old rustic building.

"How are we going to explore this village in a storm? Jerry asked.

"We'll walk in rain parkas, and if necessary, come back to the van if our bodies become chilled."

Soon, Jerry and Delilah moved thorugh narrow streets, dashed in and out of art shops then entered a quaint restaurant for hot soup and French bread.

"I'm warming up," Jerry said. "But I'm ready to move on."

"OK, we'll drive through the mountains to Apt, the capital of the Luberon Valley. I believe it's a town of ten thousand people."

"Anything to see?"

"No, we'll drive through, cross the valley, then climb toward the mountains to find a B and B in St. Saturnin les Apt. This is old village sits in the middle of high ridge under the ruins of a castle."

Later, while driving through mountainous terrain, a sign appeared on the side of the road. It read: Bonneaux.

"What is Bonneaux?" Jerry asked.

"It's a perched village built in layers. On a clear day, we would have been able to see all the other perched towns in the Luberon."

"This storm will probably block all the views from the top. Let's pass on it."

They continued their northward journey in the rain, passed through the bustling town of Apt then sped toward St. Saturnin les apt while driving beside green vineyards.

Jerry pointed. "Look at that red soil. It must give the grapes a wonderful flavor."

In the distance, a jagged brown cliff reached upward, and, it seemed, almost touched thick black clouds billowing downward from the sky. A tall white cross hung over a black smudge in the saddle— St. Saturnin les Apt.

"There it is," Delilah said. "We'll be there shortly."

Moving forward, climbing continuously, they soon reached the old village, parked their van near a rest home then walked up a steep road to the town's main street and found medieval buildings.

Starting beside an old church with a well and huge cross, they walked on what appeared to be the hamlet's only commercial street. A large blue plaque, rested on the wall of one of the buildings. It read: Here, resistance fighters gave their lives to save the inhabitants of St. Saturnin les Apt.

"What do you think happened here?" Delilah asked.

"The Nazi probably threatened to kill everyone in town if the resistance fighters didn't surrender. Those men must have been slaughtered."

Moving on, they passed narrow shops sandwiched into dilapidated buildings. A butcher displayed beautifully carved meats under a glass counter and helped a customer with her purchase. People squeezed vegetables in small shops, moved in and out of a bakery to purchase loaves of French bread and children lined up for pastries. Two grocery stores, filled with items for kitchens, had many patrons buying goods, and men lounged in chairs outside in a bar. At the end of the road, two small hotels faced each other. They poked their heads into one and found a gourmet restaurant with glass windows that exposed a spectacular view of the Luberon Valley.

"Let's come back here for dinner," Delilah suggested. Then, she grabbed Jerry's hand, crossed the street, entered the other hotel and spoke with the owner. "We need a B and B."

The woman spoke into a telephone then said to Delilah, "Wait outside. A man from village will take you home and show rooms. He'll charge 50 euros."

Jerry and Delilah walked to their van then drove behind the Frenchman to his house where they unloaded gear into a small adjacent cottage. They rested, dressed for dinner then drove back to the town's commercial street and walked to the hotel positioned on the edge of the ridge. After walking through a dark hallway, and passing the reception desk, they opened a glass door that revealed a beautiful lounge and bar. Beyond, floor-to-ceiling glass windows circled a group of small tables and the recorded voice of a French singer filled the air.

After sitting at a table and savoring the view of the Luberon Valley and mountains beyond, a tall man with a mustache came to greet them.

"I'm owner and chef," he said.

"Delilah shook his hand. "How do you survive in this small village?

We have fine reputation in Apt and entire Luberon Valley. Customers come for good food and great views. I suggest the chicken dish. It comes with a special sauce, rice and sautéed vegetables. White wine or red?

"Two white wines please."

The man departed, and Jerry held Delilah's hand and while gazing at the valley in the fading light. "What are you plans for tomorrow?"

"Tall mountains surround this ridge. It is named, Plateau de Vacluse."

"We're cycling in the mountains?"

"Yes. In the morning, we'll leave the van in the small village of Murs then cycle up to the Col du Murs."

"A col in the Luberon?"

"Surprizingly, yes. It rises to 6,200 feet and provides spectacular scenery of the entire area. We will, however, need to dress as warm as possible. It's going to be cold—really cold."

The chef served the wine and brought appetizers—green olives, small slices of French bread, oil for dipping and a bowl of ground chickpeas.

"Cover bread with paste," he said.

Slowly, darkness engulfed the Luberon Valley as Jerry and Delilah sipped wine and munched appetizers. They enjoyed dinner, topped it off with thick black coffee, and then, with regret, left the restaurant and walked on the blackened road to their van for the drive to their rented room.

Dawn arrived without a trace of clouds, and after a light breakfast, Jerry and Delilah slipped double sweaters over their cycling jerseys, pulled on tights then drove northward on a road that rose steeply through the hills. In a little while, they reached Murs, a small village of 30 or 40 old buildings. Off to the side of the road, they noticed what appeared to be an important winery.

After parking their van next to a gas station and extracting their bikes, they placed wool hats under their helmets, pulled wool mits over their gloves, fitted rain parkas over their chests, then cycled away from Murs, uphill.

The path rose, steeply, twisted from side to side on long sweeping switchbacks, and periodically, it looped near the edge of the ridge where the terrain fell downward for thousands of feet exposing the beauty of the Luberson Valley and tall purple mountains.

Jerry pulled to the edge of the precipice. "This is a breathtaking vista."

Soon, they approached a crossing road that angled sharply downhill. A sign read: Gordes, 8 kilometers. They turned their gaze backward and noticed an elderly couple, cycling without helmets, turning down the road.

"Shall we follow them on that plunge to Gordes?" Jerry asked.

"I think that route will be too steep on the return," Delilah replied. "We'll visit that stunning perched village another day. Its architecture and panoramic vistas make it a huge tourist attraction."

The road continued swinging back and forth—first to the hills, and then back to the rim of the cliff with its breathtaking views of the Luberon. Eventually, Delilah decided to rest beneath some trees, eat power bars, and drink fluids while catching their breaths.

Delilah rose from the ground and mounted her bike. "Saddle up. Let's keep climbing. We can't be too far from the Col."

They continued the slow ascent, riding side by side, and then, up ahead, noticed cyclists milling about a plateau. On approaching the group, it appeared they wore Italian jerseys. They pedaled onward and were amazed to find that the Italians had climbed a long steep grade.

"My God," Jerry exclaimed. "Look what these bikers accomplished."

Delilah tried speaking with one of the group. "Where have you come from?"

"Venaskque! Venasque!"

"Where is Venasque?" Jerry asked.

"It's at the bottom of the plateau. Let's ride back to Murs."

"Sure, let's go."

Jerry and Delilah turned their bikes, grabbed the drops of their handlebars, clicked shoes into pedals, cocked their head upward and began cycling. Faster and faster, faster and faster, they swept from side to side on the mountain while enjoying spectacular landscapes and soon reached the van.

Jerry kissed Delilah's lips. "That was wonderful. What's next?"

"Let's eat lunch at that other hotel then change into hiking clothes for a trek to the ruins of the castle above St. Saturnin les Apt.

"That sounds great—I'm starving."

Jerry and Delilah entered the restaurant, savored a quick lunch then returned to their room to dress in shorts and hiking boots. After parking their van, they walked up a steep road to reach the church and found an old staircase rising toward the ruins.

On stone steps smoothed thin over hundreds of years, they began the climbing on the exposed face of the ridge that fell towards the valley several thousand feet below. Jerry grabbed Delilah's arm.

"Be careful. One misstep and we're dead."

They scaled higher and higher, the vista became more expansive, and eventually, reached the top of the ridge, opened an iron gate and entered a triangular courtyard in front of the ruins. The ruins of the castle held an ancient wooden door with a rusted metal ring in its center. They walked about the grounds, peered over the precipice on the other side, and noticed a large lake far below.

"This must be the reservoir for the village," Jerry suggested.

They moved to the tip of the triangular courtyard, peered over the edge, and there, far below, St. Saturnin les Apt stretched out before their eyes, embraced by multicolored tile roofs, ancient, caring and eternal.

Soon, Jerry and Delilah carefully descended the ancient stone steps. Down, down, they went as the green landscape of the Luberon Valley stretched out before their eyes. Before long, they reached their van, returned to their room then rested and waited for darkness and the dinner hour.

"Let's try the restaurant where we ate lunch," Delilah suggested. "It's informal."

Jerry and Delilah seated themselves at a small table near the windows as the waitress approached them with a caraf of red wine and a long roll of hot French bread wrapped in a white napkin. She smiled. "No menu."

"No menu," Delilah echoed. "This is going to be interesting. I bet the dinner will be extraordinary."

Soon, the waitress delivered a plate with pieces of tomato topped by mozzarella cheese, dripping with olive oil. Immediately, Jerry and Delilah placed the cheese and tomatoes on pieces of French bead and ate while sipping wine. Jerry smiled. "This is delicious."

"By and by, the waitress served steaming bowls of soup on the table and said, "Lentil."

"Jerry beamed. "Wow, this is wonderful. What is this interesting flavor? It's great."

"It's basil. The soup must have been simmered for hours in basil leaves."

Presently, the main dish of the evening arrived, and it appeared to be pieces of beef with a side dish of candied carrots.

"What is it?" Jerry asked.

"Boiled beef," the waitress answered.

"Boiled beef?"

"Taste it Jerry," Delilah instructed. "They cooked the meat until it tender."

"It's wonderful. It's wonderful."

The waitress cleared the table, served a steaming pot of coffee, and in a few minutes presented flan—a delicate custard topped with caramelized sugar.

"This is delicious," Jerry said. "What are your plans for the morning?"

"We're cycling from here to the perched red village of Roussillon."

"A red village?"

"Yes, the entire area is filled with red clay, and of course, all the structures in the town have a reddish hue. It should be beautiful. Also, we'll visit Joucas, a stone village that has become an artist colony. We might find something unusual to buy."

Arm in arm, Jerry and Delilah walked out of the restaurant, then drove to their small room, and just before bed, stepped onto their porch and watched the moon hanging over the Luberon Valley. Jerry sighed. "I can't believe my joy."

The following morning, Jerry and Delilah dressed in bright yellow windbreakers then cycled with a deliberate pace through the main street of St. Saturnin les Apt where its citizens gave them curious glances. At the end of the road, a sign read: Roussillon 20 kilometers. They turned right, sped down the ridge, and, in a little while, found themselves riding on narrow road beside young green vines that extended through the valley cycling above. With almost no traffic, they felt happy and serene.

"This is wonderful," Jerry yelled. "I feel my body becoming part of valley and vineyards."

They cycled onward, and before long, saw a tall narrow mountain in the distance—Roussillon; and its red hue became apparent during their approach. Now, the sod and rocks became bright red as they climbed on a narrow undulating road.

Finally, the reddish town rose above them, and soon, they reached a viewing area and relished the sight of the red stone village. Looking below, they enjoyed the vista of brownish red cliffs and boulders hanging over the green valley, all guarded by purple mountains in the distance.

Shortly, they pushed their bikes up a steep road to the center of town and began entering small quaint shops. The painters, potters, wood craftsmen all greeted them with enthusiasm. After reaching a small narrow street filled with small boutiques, they found an artist painting in the style of Vincent Van Gogh. He demanded thousands of dollars for his canvases.

"Vincent Van Gogh is dead," Jerry declared. "But his technique lives on. It seems like total plagiarism to paint using his style. I find it disturbing."

Jerry and Delilah continued pushing their bikes upward, and then, on a high point of the village, found a restaurant with a terrace extending outward toward the valley. They enjoyed lunch and Delilah stood up and stretched. "Let's saddle up and ride to Joucas. It's not far away. I want to see art in that stone hamlet."

They cycled downhill, and after less then one hour, saw Joucas rising out of the vineyards, dark, and mysterious and foreboding. But the steep road forced them off their bikes and they pushed their machines beside a small grocery store, rested and enjoyed soft drinks. Then, they walked up a narrow path covered with time worn stones. Low slung grey rock buildings, hundreds of years old, closed in the path on each side. They found a pottery shop with interesting lamps, another with copper works, and one with huge watercolor canvases with scenes of vineyards, mountains and fields of lavender. They noticed smoke rising from one courtyard and enter with curiosity. A beautiful young woman, with long black hair, stood over a smoldering garbage can. The shop itself had shelves lined with coal-black vases.

"Is this Japanese Raku pottery?" Delilah asked.

"Modified Raku."

"Modified Raku? What is that?"

In Japan, the black glazes are kept secret and are too difficult to reproduce. Here, I've blacken the red-hot pottery by pulling them out of the kiln then placing them on a stand inside a can with fresh straw that immediately burns. The black ash fuses to the clay but doesn't touch the glazed designs on each piece."

"These works are stunning. I would like to buy that clam shell vase with the night scenes. Do you have a name for it?

"I call it moonlight on the lake."

"Do you ship?"

"Yes, all over the world."

"How much?"

"One hundreds and twenty five dollars."

Delilah extended her visa card. "OK. I'll buy it."

They left the shop, walked upward on smooth stone steps, peeked into another courtyard, and found a portly middle-aged man, covered with dust, retreating down a ladder. He answered in English.

"You're an American," Delilah declared.

"Yes."

"You have interesting sculptures made of metal and stone."

"Thank you."

"Why do you work in this isolated village? How can you live in the middle of nowhere?"

"I haven't banished myself into exile. I'm not isolated. Tourists from all over the world visit me in Joucas. People like you, ask about my life and buy art. And why, may I ask, are you in Joucas?"

"I'm a nurse. I've decided, for a while, to step away from the world."

"Searching for the meaning of life?"

"Yes."

"Searching for God?"

"I don't know."

"And you sir. Why are you in Joucas? What do you do in the States?

"I'm a physician. I've just recovered from Alzheimer's disease."

"Recovered from Alzheimer's disease?"

"Yes."

"God must have rested his hand on your shoulder."

"Yes. God rested his hand on my shoulder and my memory returned."

"I know it might sound weird but Joucas could be the center of the earth. In many ways, its like Delphi, in Greece. Here, there is beauty in every bend in the road and in every curve of the stones in this village. This place might be a monastery and I might be a monk. And yes, I feel the presence of God in this village and create sculptures. In Joucas, at sunset, a strange orange light gathers everywhere and you feel something special in your soul."

"Are you the oracle of Joucas?" Deliah asked in a whispered voice.

"I'm not sure. But, I'll say this: Art endures while all life fades away. Buildings crumble but art remains eternal. That is why I live and work in Joucas."

"I would like to buy that small statue on the table. Can you ship it?"

"Sure."

"How much.?"

"One hundred dollars."

Soon, Jerry and Delilah left the shop and pushed their bikes upward until reaching a high flat area that overlooked the valley. Far in the distance, tall purple mountains guarded its treasure.

Jerry sighed. "This is an interesting but terribly isolated village. I couldn't exist in a place like this. It's completely cut off from the rest of the world."

"Maybe that is the reason people live here. This is a spooky wonderful village."

Directly, Jerry and Delilah descended the steep steps of Joucas, cycled away, entered a small road winding through the vineyards, climbed the ridge back to St. Saturnin les Apt., reached their B and B, rested and waited for darkness.

"I'm ready to move on in the morning," Delilah declared. "Let's become, for one day, regular tourists. I want to visit the perched village of Gordes, drive to see the interesting town of St. Remy de Provence and enjoy the Roman ruins at Les Baux. It sits on a high ridge. Then, we'll drive toward the Rhone river and sleep in a mas deep in the vineyards.

"What is a mas?"

"It's an old farm house, hundreds of years old."

Early the next morning, as the sun rose over the Luberon Valley, Jerry and Delilah drove slowly through the empty streets of St. Saturnin les Apt on their way to another beautiful village.

Jerry waved his hand out the window. "Good-by St. Saturnin."

Drive toward the Col du Murs," Delilah instructed. "We'll turn on that high mountain for the road then descend into Gordes."

In awhile, the van rose onto a plateau, and about a mile from the col, Jerry steered down a steep path, and with each switchback, the green Luberon Valley below became more beautiful.

"We should have cycled here after climbing to the Col," Jerry said. "This is a spectacular plunge."

Soon, they passed a few modern homes, a fancy restaurant, and then, in the distance, saw the tiled roof of a chateau. They parked the van in a designated area, pulled on heavy sweaters, walked downhill into Gordes and began entering small art shops, here and there.

They entered an interesting boutique displaying enormous vases, wandered about, then sat at a table in the back where the owner served coffee and desserts. A floor-to-ceiling glass window exposed a lovely courtyard filled with colorful plants that emerged from gigantic stand-up urns with interesting designs.

"What a charming place," Delilah declared. "This earthenware mart has a small restaurant and an enchanting garden, too."

They continued exploring the village, visited the chateau and found an artist painting watercolor scenes of Provence.

"She's the best," Delilah exclaimed. "Look, these delicate flowers seem real. I'll buy a matched pair for my kitchen."

The painter took Delilah's order. "You'll receive your art in one month."

They moved on and explored the sheer cliffs surrounding the village, examined colorful rock formations and stared out at the valley below.

"The Nazi army almost destroyed Gordes," Jerry said.

"I know, the French resistance used this village as a base."

"Let's move on to St. Remy," Jerry said. "This is going to be a long day. I hope we reach the house in the vineyard before dark."

Jerry and Delilah descended into the valley on a long winding road, and intermittently, looked back in awe as the village of Gorges receded behind them. Soon, they drove through small towns and approached the outskirts of St. Remy on a road lined by closely packed plane trees. Narrow naked trunks soared toward the sky with branches that spread upward like inverted umbrellas.

"What a breathtaking entrance into St. Remy," Delilah said. "I've seen this spooky route in a movie. It could have been in a Bergman film or that French masterpiece, *A man and a woman.*"

Eventually, Jerry and Delilah found a parking area, joined a throng of people enjoying market day. They repeatedly sqeezed themselves between packed sidewalks, stalls and buildings.

"Watch your wallet," Delilah said.

Tradesmen offered every type of ware—lace goods, leather products, sweaters, pants, shoes, paintings, pottery, fowl, fish, meats and all variety of vegetables.

"This street holds a complete department store," Delilah said. "I'm buying this black scarf with colorful sequins. How do you like it."

"It's beautiful. You look like a Spanish dancer with that scarf wrapped around your neck."

"Delilah, come here. Taste the strawberries. They are the most strawberry strawberries on the face of this earth. Taste the oranges. Come taste the cherry tomatoes. They are tart—real tart."

"Slow down, Jerry. You'll spoil your appetite for lunch."

They stopped at a vendor selling olive oil and began tasting the yellow liquid on the freshly cut slices of French bread.

"This is wonderful. Let's buy a bottle."

"Jerry, I'm not sure we should do that. If the bottle breaks in a backpack our clothes will be ruined."

"Where do they grow the olives?" Jerry asked the vendor.

"Les Baux. The best olive trees in France are in Les Baux."

In a little while, Jerry and Delilah stopped at a stall where a man sold white wine from the Luberon Valley, and after filling small plastic cups, they continued strolling and sipping the vintage then approached two musicians playing soothing hypnotic music. The man, dressed in a colorful Peruvian shawl, played a long wooden flute while a young woman with long blond hair, plucked a flat homemade string instrument like a zither. Transfixed by the music, they felt lifted into the sublime.

"Do you have a name for this interesting music?" Jerry asked.

"Solstice D'ete."

"The summer solstice," Delilah echoed.

Jerry started to walk away, but returned and bought a disc. "Delilah, we can play this exotic music while making love at night. It's perfect."

"Come on sexy, let's move on."

Moving with the crowd, Jerry and Delilah ambled down the road inspecting a variety of goods, but then, a short distance away, noticed a young woman standing alone. Dressed in a thin black evening gown with shoestring straps, her long black hair cascaded over bare shoulders white as snow. In a melodic French voice, she read poetry behind a small table filled with sheets of paper. Her voice, simple and pure, shocked Jerry to his roots. A tall black hat stood on the ground partially filled with currency.

"French or English?" she asked as they approached.

"English," Jerry said while throwing euros into the hat.

The woman handed Jerry a piece of paper and slowly read her

poem "Hearts and souls."

Unhurriedly at first, and then with increasing pace, she spoke about a lost boyfriend, a broken heart and how to listen to echoes of the soul to find true love. The words and phrases, soft and eloquent, floated over Jerry and Delilah like a gentle soothing mist.

Jerry smiled. "That was really beautiful. Delilah, let's find an outdoor restaurant for lunch. I want to find a table where we can watch interesting people."

Presently, they worked their way through the throng, found a small café on the Remy's main avenue, enjoyed simple pasta dishes, coffee and desserts. Delilah stood up. "We're off to visit the Roman ruins at Les Baux. This 2,000-year-old fortress sits on a high ridge, and we'll need to hike to reach this historic site."

Before long, Jerry and Delilah found themselves driving past fields of olive trees, reached a parking area, then began hiking up a steep paved road.

"Let's pass all the shops," Delilah instructed. "Today, we're on a tight schedule and must reach the farm house before nightfall."

Finally, at the summit of the ridge, they saw the ancient fortifications—a mass of jumbled pink stones rising toward the sky. Delilah climbed among the thick colorful rocks as a fierce wind whipped her long auburn hair all about. "Shoot a picture. I want proof my presence in these ancient Roman ruins. My friends at the hospital will love this shot."

Jerry snapped a photo then moved to the edge of the precipice and peered out in the distance shielding the sun from the eyes with his hand. "I can see the Mediterranean Ocean. Also, there is a brown smudge on the horizon. I bet that's Marseilles. The Romans placed a fort on this ridge because they could see in all directions. I feel good here—the wind, the view and the primitive nature of this place is exhilarating. Let's return one day and hike in this location. OK?"

Delilah continued climbing among the rocky debris and Jerry followed. "Don't fall," she warned. "Our trip will be ruined if you break a leg."

Finally, Delilah returned to the ridge. "Jerry, this is great, but it is time to leave for the farm house. I"ll call the owner when we approach the area so she can deliver the keys. The building is several hundred years old and it rents for the price of a room—50 euros."

"How did you find this place?"

"On the Internet."

"Is it near a town?"

"I don't think so."

"Where will we eat?"

"I don't know. Our stay in the vineyards will be an adventure."

"Is this house in the middle of nowhere?"

"Probably. We'll move on the next morning if the accommodations are poor. Our next house is on the Western side of the Rhone river.

Several hours later, Jerry and Delilah found themselves driving on a narrow paved highway surrounded by miles of young green vines; and then, off on the right, a dirt road appeared with a plaque. It read: Mas Coocherou.

The van caused a cloud of dust as they navigated the thread-like route that twisted through the vineyard. A squat house covered with a multicolored tiled roof appeared in the distance, and soon, they noticed a late model sports car beside the building. A beautiful young woman stepped out of the car, dressed like a fashion model.

"I'm the owner," she said in a thick French accent. "We don't live here. My husband and I bought this farm only for the vines. They give special flavor to the wines in our vats. You sleep here for 50 euros."

"We'll try this house for one night and stay on if we like it," Delilah replied.

"OK, call me and place keys in door if you leave."

"Thank you," Jerry said while handing the woman a 50-euro note.

The woman offered keys, turned, entered the car then sped away in a haze of dust.

Jerry smiled and waved. "That was a beautiful rich woman. The owners of these vineyards must be millionaires."

Alone in the vineyard, in the middle of nowhere, Delilah approached the door of the old farm house with hesitation and some trepidation. "This is going to be an adventure."

They turned the key in the lock, pushed open the heavy wooden door, entered a cramped hallway, pulled a light switch, and then, immediately faced a stone staircase that steeply rose toward the second floor.

"We'll need hiking sticks to climb these stairs," Jerry said with a sarcastic tone.

Moving to the left they entered a huge room with two narrow beds. A pair of mosquito nets hung from the ceiling and an enormous bathtub filled the end of the chamber. Promptly, they rotated to the right and stepped into a large dining room occupied by a long oak table, high-backed chairs and a floor-to-ceiling wooden cabinet with glass doors that exhibited dishes and cups. Just beyond, a stove and refrigerator filled a small kitchen. They returned to the hallway and began to climb the stone staircase.

"Hold the wall with your hand," Jerry instructed. "You'll break your skull if you fall."

At the top of the stairs, they turned left, opened a door and found a large room with a four-poster bed completely covered with mosquito netting. They returned to the staircase, spun right, then stepped into a large room with soft couches lining two walls. A large four-poster bed rested against a wall under mosquito netting.

Jerry smiled. "I think this will be an interesting romantic evening. I've never made love in a bed like this."

They entered the bath area and found an enormous open shower stall with a colorful mosaic tiled floor. Two long golden shower heads extended toward the center from opposite walls.

"A person standing in this shower will be blasted by hot water from both sides at the same time," Delilah said with a smile.

"Let's shower together in this lovely place after making love in the four-poster bed," Jerry said. "I can't wait to hold you in the water. Our bodies will fuse in the steam and become a single thing."

"You know, Jerry, you're a really sexy man."

Jerry and Delilah opened the door to a separate toilet room, and to their amazement, found a large oil painting facing the commode. A French general, dressed in a splendid blue uniform, stood in front of a desk, quill in hand.

"This is a real spooky house," Delilah declared. "But we must leave at once to find a restaurant in the nearest town. I don't want to drive through this isolated vineyard in the black of night."

Immediately, they left the farmhouse, retreated on the narrow dusty road, then turned north on a paved highway beside vast green vineyards searching for a town.

"Who could possibly drink all the wine made from these vines?" Jerry asked.

"Farmers from the Rhone Valley ship products all over the world."

Suddenly, a tractor slowed the northward movement of their van, and while waiting, they watched, with concern, as a man, dressed in head-to-toe rubber suit, drove a tanker truck on a narrow paths between the vines. Like a moving fountain, both sides of the truck sprayed yellow liquid onto fresh green leaves.

"Oh, God," Jerry said. "He's drenching the vines with insecticide. Chemical poisons will contaminate anyone drinking wines made from these grapes. This is terrible! In the future, I'm only drinking wine from organic vineyards."

Delilah frowned. "I'm not drinking these wines. Organic vineyards in France are called 'Bio.' We'll get their names in the restaurant."

Eventually, Jerry and Delilah found a café in a small town and enjoyed a simple evening meal.

"We're definitely moving in the morning," Delilah declared. "We'll cross the Rhone river and sleep in a modern house with an outdoor pool. It's in a small town named Serviers just west of Uzes."

"Why Serviers?"

"This small village is positioned 20 miles north of Nimes, a city with Roman ruins. We'll cycle into that interesting town the day after tomorrow."

"Let's scout the area before giving our commitment. OK?"

"Sure, but I'm reasonably satisfied that the next accommodations will be great. The owner has a small cottage next to his home."

The next day, Jerry and Delilah loaded their van, left keys in the door of the mas then drove off for a visit the winery's chateau.

"Let's taste a little wine from this vineyard," Delilah said. "Then, we'll find breakfast in a village on the way to the next house on the other side of the Rhone river."

Soon, using excellent instructions from the owner of the mas, they arrived at a chateau that suddenly rose out of the vast fields of vines. A young woman greeted them in a reception area and lined up four bottles of red wine.

"These are years 1999 through 2003, she said. "They taste slightly different but all are excellent."

"We stayed overnight in the mas," Delilah announced. "That was an interesting experience."

"The woman stepped into the office, and spoke with the owner of the winery who came out and warmly greeted Jerry and Delilah. "You like mas? You sleep well?"

"Your mas is quite old and unique," Jerry replied. "We thank you for the bottle of wine left on the dining room table. It tasted wonderful."

"You speak English without much accent," Delilah added.

"Years ago. I studied with Paul Mason at his winery in California then returned to run our family's business. We blend our wine with grapes from nearby vineyards, but vines surrounding the mas produce grapes with a unique flavor that adds to the character of the product in the vats. Oak barrels finish off the taste, and after one year, the wine is sold to the best restaurants in Europe."

"How do you know when to harvest?"

"We measure the sugar content in the grapes, and when it is high, send automatic equipment through the fields to pick them after several days of dry weather. Last year, we harvested at night to place cool wine in our vats."

Delilah lifted a glass of wine sitting in front of a bottled labeled 2000. This wine is great. It's delicious."

"Wine from that year was one of the best", the owner declared. "Sugar levels in grapes remained high with weeks of uninterrupted sunshine. Each wine captures year-long effects of the sunshine, rain, temperature and the soil. It's all there in the taste of the wine. Our vineyards produce excellent wine each year because of the red clay soil. But in 2000, all conditions produced an outstanding wine that has received rave reviews."

Jerry bought a bottle of wine labeled 2000 then followed the owner on a tour of the facility. In the next building, he showed them a floor-to-ceiling holding vat, automatic bottling equipment and stacks of oak barrels aging the wine.

"How do you preserve the liquid in the vats?" Jerry asked.

"Wine contains natural sulfites, but for safety, we added a small extra dose. We've never had a problem with bacterial contamination."

Jerry and Delilah followed the owner into the green lawn surrounding the chateau, enjoyed the beautiful gardens then thanked him before entering their van.

In a while, they crossed the Rhone river, passed into the small town of Remoulins, enjoyed breakfast in a small café, continued on, drove near the cut-off road to the famous Pont du Gard then entered the old town of Uzes and found themselves surrounded by heavy traffic.

Delilah frowned. "It's another market day. They usually finish at noon so there is no point in stopping. We're searching for Serviers, a few miles to the west. I've asked for a three-night stay."

"Why three nights?"

"Tomorrow, we'll cycle to Nimes to visit the Roman ruins, and on the following day, ride to the Pont du Gard, the 2000-year-old aqueduct. This schedule requires three nights. Then, we'll drive to airport in Marseille, return the van, sleep in a hotel then prepare for the flight to Florence the next morning."

"Only four more nights in France? It's a shame. We've had a wonderful experience here."

"Yes, our adventure has been nice but we must reach Tuscany before tourists flood the area."

Directly, Jerry and Delilah entered Serviers, passed homes that appeared to be hundreds of years old, then turned onto a small road surrounded by vineyards. They found their house completely sheltered by tall hedges and noticed the owner busily clipping bushes.

"Welcome. Welcome," he said with a deep foreign accent.

"We'll stay three nights."

"Fine. Fine. I show little house. Everyone like little house."

"You don't have a French accent," Jerry said.

"I Swiss. I retired from Zurich to peaceful Serviers. Come. Come. I show house."

Jerry and Delilah followed the man behind his home, walked past an outdoor pool with a cabana, admired the vineyards in the distance then entered the kitchen of the small cottage. Next, they stepped into a sitting room with sofas as the owner pulled a curtain that revealed floor-to-ceiling glass windows. Then, he disclosed two small bedrooms.

"Beds good," he said while pounding the mattresses. Three nights. Three hundreds euros."

"OK," Jerry answered while pulling bills from his wallet. "It looks good. Where can we eat dinner?"

"Restaurants no good in Serviers. You shop super marche. Food wonderful."

"OK," Delilah said. "We'll buy food in the super marche and cook in the kitchen. Tell me. What is that high hill in the distance? We're cycling to Nimes in the morning."

"Small mountain with gorge."

"Really! What comes after that on the road to Nimes."

"Vineyards. Vineyards. Vineyards."

"And beyond?"

"High bridge over beautiful river."

"Really. That sounds wonderful. And beyond the river?"

"A mountain pass."

"Really. That sounds great. And beyond the mountain pass?"

"Only four miles to Nimes," he said while presenting keys to the cottage.

Jerry and Delilah unloaded their van then sped off to shop in the super marche on the outskirts of Serviers.

"This looks like a modern super market found in the United States," Delilah declared as they approached the area. "We'll need food for three dinners, four breakfasts and two lunches. We can make sandwiches with ham and cheese? Is that OK?"

"Sure. I'm not hard to please."

They entered the super marche and found they needed a key to extract a shopping cart. A woman at a desk forced Delilah to give her name and address.

Off to the left, half the store seemed devoted to dry goods, while on the right, an entire wall held mounds of fresh fruits and vegetables.

In the center, clerks in white coats manned a circular refrigerated area and cut cheeses from all over France. Beyond, at the back of the store, sales women stood in front of a refrigerated glass cases that held chicken, beef and pork. And scattered all about, huge carts, filled with ice, displayed all types of fresh fish. In the corner of the store, machines held long rods that roasted chicken under hot lamps.

"Let's shop strategically," Delilah said. "For breakfast, we'll buy coffee, milk, cereal, French bread, juice, jam and butter. For lunch, we'll purchase ham and cheese for sandwiches, and for dinner, we'll buy fresh salmon and pasta then use the rotisserie chicken for the other two meals. Is that OK?"

"Sure. That sounds great. Go, Delilah, go."

Before long, they finished shopping then returned to the house and unloaded their groceries.

Jerry stood in the patio and pointed toward the fields. "Let's go for a walk in the vineyards behind the house. I see a path that circles through the vines."

Directly, Jerry and Delilah pulled on hiking boots and shorts then began strolling through the area under a warm afternoon sun. Workers in the fields busily tied young green branches to wires that stretched out for miles.

Suddenly, behind them, they heard sound of hoof beats, and quickly, they stepped into the vines as a huge black horse bore down on them. High above the animal, a tall man, stripped bare to the waist, rode in the saddle with sweat dripping down his chest.

"Bonjour," he yelled while rushing past. "Bonjour. Bonjour."

"There rides the owner of these vineyards," Jerry exclaimed. "He's surveying his vines on horseback. To watch him riding here is to see a brief capsule of this man's life. Did you see the pleasure on his face? Did you see his status? He more than an owner. He's a patriarch. I bet this vineyard has been in his family for generations. What a life! Grow grapes. Make wines. Ride through the vineyards on a magnificent animal. What a life!"

"You're jealous."

"I am indeed. I want to ride through these vineyards on a wild black stallion with sunshine on my skin and the wind in my face."

"Let's go back. I need to prepare dinner and examine the map for tomorrow's ride to Nimes."

By and by, Jerry and Delilah grilled fresh salmon on an outdoor grill, enjoyed hot noodles and washed everything down with a delicious local wine graciously provided by the owner of the cottage.

"Let's go to bed early," Delilah suggested. "Tomorrow, we'll have a long ride with a great deal of climbing. We can prepare sandwiches after breakfast."

In the morning, they pulled on yellow windbreakers to ward off the chill, and almost immediately, began climbing toward the small mountain in the distance.

Soon, they found themselves riding beside white limestone cliffs, while on the right side of the road, the terrain fell sharply off into a deep gorge filled with huge boulders and green bushes. A small meandering stream rushed through at the bottom.

"This is gorgeous," Jerry exclaimed. "But it tough climbing so early in the morning."

Before long, they reached the summit of the hill, and then, without delay, swiftly descended onto a narrow road that twisted beside vast acres of vines that stretched out in all directions.

Relaxed, they continued to cycle on this serene path with the morning sun in their faces, and soon, reached Bourdic, the first village on the map. They approached a wine cooperative surrounded by cars and trucks. In front of the building, vendors sold fruit, vegetables and jams.

They parked their bikes and Delilah bought a jar of fig jam while Jerry sampled fresh nougat bars filled with almonds.

Jerry smiled. "Come taste these slices. They're wonderful."

"Load up on nougat bars. We'll need fuel for our long ride to Nimes."

They entered the building and found people lined up at a long bar tasting wines, while on the other side of the room, customers filled gallon jugs with wine from long hoses that extended from the wall.

"This is amazing," Jerry declared. "People are filling containers with wine like fueling gas tanks in cars."

"Don't drink the wine," Delilah advised. "We'll need all of our energy for climbing today."

In a while, Jerry and Delilah mounted bikes, and now, fully loaded with jam and nougat bars, continued cycling in a southerly direction toward Nimes. They entered the small hamlet of St. Anstasie, enjoyed pastries at a bakery, and watched in amazement, as fashionably dressed men and women emerged from houses that appeared hundreds of years old. Luxurious cars appeared everywhere.

"Owners of these vineyards appear quite wealthy," Jerry said. "This is a rich vibrant community."

Continuing to cycle on a narrow route between the vines, they passed through the small villages of Roussau then reached a high bridge rising above a deep gorge. Several hundred of feet below, a fast moving river carried people in bright yellow rafts and the beaches seemed filled with sunbathers. Delilah held the railing of the span as the wind blew her auburn hair. "This gorge is spectacular."

Soon, they cycled on and almost immediately began climbing. "We're starting to scale the mountain pass leading to Nimes," Delilah yelled.

"When can we eat nougat bars?"

"At the summit. We'll pedal hard then rest at the top of the mountain."

Jerry and Delilah continued climbing, and before long, found themselves riding beside land reserved for French war games. On each side of this road, warning signs read: Danger Live shells. Do not enter.

"We can't stop," Jerry yelled. "We'll be blown up by the French army."

After awhile, they reached the top of the pass and a driver in a passing car assured them that the road led to Nimes, only four miles away. They rested, enjoyed jam, nougat bars, and energy drinks.

"Let's saddle up and ride to Nimes," Delilah said. "It's Sunday. I don't believe we'll face heavy traffic."

They sped downhill, and on reaching a major highway, stopped to evaluate their position.

"We must turn left," Delilah said, "and ride eastward toward Nimes, find the old city, examine the Roman ruins, enjoy lunch, then cycle northward on route 979 in the direction of Uzes. Eventually, we'll find the road that leads through the vineyards to Serviers."

They saddled up, cycled through increasing traffic into Nimes, and Delilah repeatedly asked for instructions, "Old city? Old city?" she shouted to drivers as they stopped at traffic lights. All fingers pointed straight ahead, and eventually, they found themselves near a huge park filled with interesting Roman statutes.

"This must be Jardin de la Fontaine."

They entered the flat area filled with benches and tables, examined ancient figuerines then rested beside an old stone wall with sculptures. A narrow canal, filled with flowing water, provided a pleasant setting for lunch.

"This water comes from a huge spring," Delilah announced. "Let's eat here. We can watch the tourists too."

They pulled out large pieces of French bead filled with thick pieces of ham and cheese as youths gathered around them to inspect their high-tech bikes.

"Jerry," Delilah said, "don't get nervous. These kids won't touch our equipment."

154

They finished their meal, bought soft drinks from a local vendor, mounted up then began cycling on the main road toward the old city. Soon, they reached a gigantic Roman administrative building that had been coverted into a library, and behind it, noticed a wide plaza, filled with outdoor restaurants where many people enjoyed eating in the afternoon sun.

Jerry and Delilah moved slowly, ever so slowly, almost like cyclists pedaling in pantomime, into the old city's narrow streets. They passed structures that appeared hundreds of years old, but to their amazement, found ground floors of buildings filled with stores selling luxurious goods. Here and there, in small alleys, people filled interesting restaurants cloaked in ambience.

"OK," Delilah said, "we've seen the old city. Now, let's find the highway leading north in the direction of Uzes. For sure, we'll need to climb out of Nimes."

They retraced their path through the old city, reached the main road and began searching for sign directing traffic to the north. "Uzes? Uzes?" Delilah asked workmen on the road.

Finally, they found a sign, turned, and immediately began climbing away from Nimes on a road filled with heavy traffic. Soon, they began cycling beside vineyards, but now, headed directly into a fierce wind. They climbed against the wind. Against the wind.

"Follow me," Jerry yelled. "I'll shield you from this blast of nature."

"Nursing home athlete becomes Lance Armstrong," Delilah shouted." "Go Jerry, go."

On a narrow shoulder on the road, with yellow windbreakers billowing in the air, they cycled toward Uzes, and after struggling for an hour, reached a narrow downhill road surrounded by a mountain on one side and a low stone wall on the other. They slowly approached Pont St. Nicholas, a bridge that spanned a deep spectacular gorge.

They crossed, stopped and watched the beautiful river below, but in a little while, mounted their bikes, turned left then biked on a side path that led deep into the vineyards. The afternoon sun drifted low toward the horizon.

"We're heading for the route leading to the wine cooperative and Serviers."

"I'm fading fast," Jerry yelled.

"Hold on, Jerry. Hold on. We'll rest and eat nougat bars at the wine coopertive. Just hold on."

Cycling uphill against the wind, they grabbed the drops of their handlebars and huddled low on their bikes, and eventually, noticed a sign for Bourdic, and soon reached the wine cooperative.

"I'm finished," Jerry announced. "I can't pedal one more stroke."

"Jerry," Delilah said, "eat nougat bars and wash your face. We don't have much further to go. Its only seven kilometers to Serviers. After climbing up that hill, we'll have a downhill ride to our house."

"OK. I'll eat one more nougat bar then mount up one last time. But please, don't drop me like you're riding in the Tour de France."

"Let's see your stuff, Lance Armstrong. We'll pedal as slowly as necessary to keep you in the saddle. You'll make it, I'm sure."

They continued on, climbed the small mountain near Serviers, then sped downhill to their house and quickly parked their bikes.

"Congratulations, Jerry, you made it back alive. Go shower while I fix dinner. You'll feel better with some food."

Jerry stripped off his clothes, showered then collapsed on the bed while Delilah cooked dinner. She heated chicken, pasta and French bread in the microwave oven, set the table, opened a bottle of wine and added a bowl of fresh strawberries and melon. Soon, Jerry returned to the kitchen.

"I feel better," he said, "but my body is wasted. I can barely move. I hope you don't expect me to perform later this evening."

"Lance, come over here and give me a kiss. You're getting stronger and I doubt that your body is finished for the day. At home, you trained for nights like this. Remember?"

"I've bought you a single white rose from the garden. It's a sensuous thing of beauty— like you."

"Jerry. You're an incurable romantic. Come. Eat your chicken. You'll feel better in a little while."

In silence, Jerry and Delilah enjoyed dinner, sipped wine and privately thought about their extraordinary cycling day to Nimes. Finally, Delilah caressed Jerry's arm. "Tomorrow, is our last riding day in France. It will be difficult to reach the Pont du Gard and return before dark. Let's go to bed early and gather our strength."

In the morning, Jerry and Delilah slipped on yellow jackets, cycled over the nearby hill, pedaled to the small village of Bourdic, and just beyond the wine cooperative turned onto a narrow road that disappeared into the vineyards.

"Are you sure this small path leads to Blauzac?"

"I saw a little sign near the ground when we turned," Delilah yelled. "Don't worry."

The lane twisted back and forth, and soon, they relaxed while riding almost on top of the vines.

Jerry beamed. "This is great. We've become part of the vineyards again."

In a little while, they entered the small town of Blauzac and noticed an unusual mixture of old buildings and modern houses; and well dressed people with late model cars moved all about. The main road split in multiple directions, and while searching for an exit to the town, they found themselves riding downhill besidemodern homes and gardens. Uncomfortable with their choice of roads, they spoke with a man watering his lawn, received instructions, climbed back up the hill then stopped again uncertain about how to leave Blauzac.

Directly, Jerry waved to a passing motorist who stopped, gave them a queer look, but then, in halting English, tried to explain the proper route toward Pont Du Gard. Immediately, they mounted up, cycled for awhile, but again felt lost.

Soon, Jerry waved down another driver, and the man stopped, looked Delilah up and down as if examining a slave on an auction block then pointed to a road in a different direction. "Sanilhac. Go Sanilhac."

Jerry grimaced. "I'm feeling uncomfortable. That man raped you with his eyes and I think we've become a spectacle in Blauzac."

"The road to Sanilhac is correct," Delilah replied. "Relax, we're on the right road to the Pont du Gard."

They began enjoying the ride beside the vineyards, and in a while, reached Sanilhac where they stopped at a bakery with an attached café. Inside, they found American hikers eagerly buying pastry.

Delilah approached a girl. "Where are you trekking?"

"We're backpacking through the forest, descending into the gorge then walking along the river. Where are you cycling?"

"The Pont du Gard. We've come from Serviers near Uzes."

Jerry bought cheese puffs and custard pies while Delilah purchase hot soup. They sat at a small table to enjoy their morning snack. "Next stop is the town of Collias," Delilah said. "A river runs through it."

Shortly, they cycled onward, and before long, reached Collias among moderate traffic. At a bridge spanning the river, they stopped and watched tourists loading into yellow rafts.

"I wonder how if feels to float down the river," Jerry asked.

"Probably, a lots of fun."

As they pedaled on, Delilah spotted an interesting hotel. "Let's stop and take a look. It has three stars dangling over the entrance. The name of this place is Le Castellas."

They entered a luxurious lobby, passed the reception desk then opened a glass door that led to a beautiful garden with tables. A menu revealed a dinner price of 100 euros. "This is a gorgeous hotel," Delilah declared. "They serve a one price dinner that must be gourmet."

"Our chef is one of the best in Europe," the bellboy announced.

"Do you need a reservation?"

"Not tonight," Jerry replied. "We're cycling to the Point du Gard."

Delilah smiled. "Let's stay here if we come back this way again."

Promptly, they turned onto a narrow path and found themselves riding among interesting dense vegetation. Along the way, they passed cherry trees, stopped, enjoyed a snack, cycled on, reached a small park and noticed one end of the Pont du Gard in the distance.

"Is it curved?" Jerry asked. "It looks like it has a slight curve from this vantage point."

"I think you're right. For some reason, the Romans built it with a curve. Perhaps this type of span is stronger than one built on a straight line."

They dismounted and began walking their bikes among a throng of people marching toward the Roman edifice that rose high above their heads with three tiers and golden stone arches.

"Look," Jerry said, "the builders left small cavities in these huge blocks for scaffolding. What a spectacular structure. It has lasted 2000 years after bringing water to Nimes but our modern buildings remain upright only for 100 years of less."

They pushed their bikes onto grassy area beside a river, pulled out sandwiches, snapped open soft drinks purchased from a local vendor then enjoyed lunch.

"This mob of tourists has partially spoiled the serenity and grandeur of the Pont du Gard," Jerry said. "In several more weeks, people won't even be able to move near this attraction."

"At least you and I have experienced the Pont du Gard and the French vineyards by bicycle. It's the best method of touring."

They rose from the grass, pushed through the crowd then entered the bike path and cycled back to Collias.

"Let's take a different route home," Delilah suggested. "I can't bear to get lost again in Blauzac. "We can ride to route 112, cross the highway near the Pont St. Nicolas, then head north beside the vineyards to Bourdic."

They cycled onward in the afternoon heat, and then, near the end to the day, with the sun almost gone, reached the wine cooperative.

"I'm wiped out again," Jerry announced. "I'll need to wash up and eat nougat bars before going on."

In a while, they mounted up, challenged the hill on the way to Serviers, and then, on the last mile, sped downhill to their house for a grateful rest.

"Let's eat dinner then get to bed early," Delilah suggested. "In the morning, we're driving to Marseilles to catch our flight to Florence."

Jerry and Delilah awoke with the rising sun, ate breakfast then drove to the airport north of Marseilles, returned the van to the rental agency, entered the Best Western hotel, packed their bikes in cardboard boxes, then rested and waited for their morning flight.

"I can't wait to visit Florence," Delilah said. "We'll enjoy the best pasta dishes in the world, visit famous art museums, examine medieval architecture then challenge the long green hills of Tuscanny."

"I can't believe we're starting the final phase of our exotic journey," Jerry said with his head down. "I've stepped off the world, and now, I don't wish to return. Let's stay and experience an endless summer. I crave the warm European sunshine on my face—it makes me happy. I need to watch your long hair billowing in the wind on downhill rides. And at night, I hunger for your tired body lying next to me. Please, let's stay and experience an endless summer. I'll delay my search for a publisher and a teaching position. This has been a gut wrenching spectacular trip. Believe me, if I die tomorrow, I'll go with a smile."

"Jerry, you're not going to die. Please, don't think about your future. Just enjoy each day, one at a time. Then, we'll remember this adventure for the rest of our lives."

Chapter Twelve

TUSCANY

Jerry and Delilah flew into Florence, and in the airport's baggage department, extracted bikes from cardboard boxes, and then, with packs on their backs, walked out into warm tuscan sunshine searching for a taxi. Soon, a large cab loaded their gear, and in a while, deposited them at the Hotel Porta Forenza near the historic district.

"I believe this hotel will store our bikes in a garage," Delilah said with satisfaction."

They wheeled their machines into the hotel's lobby where a clerk offered keys to their rooms and a code to open the door to the garage.

"We need tickets for the famous Uffizi Gallery," Delilah told the man.

"No tickets. Florence is full."

"No tickets?"

"You can see Michelangelo's David, but lines are long."

"What can we do in Florence if museums are filled with people?"

"Visit city. See architecture."

"Let's dress for cycling and check our bikes for damage," Deliah suggested. "They must be in perfect condition when we challenge the tuscan hills later in the week."

Shortly, on narrow streets near the hotel, Jerry and Delilah rode back and forth testing gears and adjusting seats and handlebars.

"I hear grinding noises during shifts," Delilah announced. "This bike must be fixed as soon as possible."

"I'll leave my Trek in the garage then find a taxi to transport your machine to a shop."

By and by, Delilah had her bike on a rack in a cycling store, and soon, a technician found a worn chain and a malfunctioning front derailleur.

"Gears shifts good with new chain," the man said.

Delilah smiled as she pushed her bike into a taxi. "Our bikes are now ready for hard cycling in Tuscany."

Feeling pleased, they returned to the hotel, showered then dressed for dinner.

Before long, they found a small family owned restaurant near the hotel, seated themselves at a small table and reviewed the menu.

"I'll order for both of us. OK."

"Sure. Sure. My life, as always, is in your hands."

The waiter approached with a large basket of fresh bread and a bowl of green olives.

"We'll have two glasses of red wine, green salads, grilled eggplants and two tomato pastas. Bring flan for desserts and black coffees too."

After dinner, Jerry and Delilah walked into the darkened historic district where the illuminated dome of the cathedral seemed to pull them forward like a powerful magnet. Delilah poked her head into a quaint restaurant. "The food smells wonderful. Tomorrow let's come back here for dinner."

"We've had a great meal," Jerry declared. "The wine tasted great, the olive oil on the salad seemed delicate and the sauce had chunks of fresh tomatoes."

"I'm going to search for the perfect tomato sauce while in Tuscany," Delilah announced. "I'll ask for the recipe."

"This is a spooky walk, but I can't wait to see the art in the bapistry."

Totally exhausted, they returned to the hotel, collapsed in bed, and before closing her eyes, Delilah kissed Jerry on the lips. "Tomorrow,

Florence will fill our souls with beautiful art."

The following day, they enjoyed a full breakfast in the hotel then began walking toward the historic district, but almost immediately, found themselves surrounded by hundreds of touring groups led by leaders holding numbered poles high in the air.

"Don't get stabbed by one of these shafts," Jerry said sarcastically. "There must be 50,000 people in the center of Florence."

"Look, the doors to the cathedral are blocked," she replied. "Try to move ahead. There must be 100,000 people trying to see the art. Do you see those interesting figuerines near the base of the dome?

"Yes. Yes. But I'm trying to find Ghiberti's Eastern Doors. Michelango said they looked like the 'gates of paradise.'"

Delilah pointed her finger. "There they are. Try to get closer."

"I can't. I can't. There are too many people here."

"Let's try to find Michelangelo's David," Delilah suggested. "It's in the museum named Galleria del Academia."

They checked their maps, walked a few blocks, but found a long line snaking around the building. Delilah frowned. "Let's return later in the day. Maybe the tourists will leave for their hotels."

"The Ponte Veechio, the famous bridge built in 1345, is an interesting sight. Let's go," Jerry suggested.

In a while, they reached the span, gazed at the river as it snaked between medieval buildings, strolled past famous shops lining the walkway, examined art on the sidewalks then passed to the other side of the bridge into old Florence. Here, they found a quaint restaurant for lunch.

"Tomato pastas, green salads followed by flan for dessert and black coffee," Delilah told the waiter.

"Will you order tomato pastas for lunch every day?" Jerry asked with a smile.

"Yes, until I find the most special sauce in all of Tuscany."

"What is that?"

"Well, it must be sweet, filled with pieces of fresh tomatoes and have a hint of tartness and spice too. I enjoyed it once in Las Vegas but didn't ask for the recipe—a big mistake."

Jerry enjoyed his lunch but the tomato pasta didn't stimulate compliments from Delilah. "Let's try to see the 'David,' she said. "If necessary, we should stay in line the rest of the afternoon."

"I agree. But I'm tired of fighting mobs of tourists. I think we should cycle out of Florence in the morning."

"OK. We'll ride out, head south, cross the beautiful Arno river, enter Chianti, the grape growing region of Tuscany, visit the town of Greve, then climb to the Villa Rossa hotel. It sits below the walled village of Radda. I'll make the arrangements later in the day."

By and by, Jerry and Delilah worked their way through the crowd on the bridge then found the museum housing Michelango's masterpiece. Fortunately, the line to the door seemed reasonable, and before long, they stood beside 'The David,' fifteen feet tall.

"This is incredible," Delilah exclaimed. "This must be the world's most wonderful piece of art."

Jerry beamed. "Look at those gorgeous muscles in the neck, thorax and torso. They appear real. Look at that face—it's a Greek Adonis. The David is not circumcised even though he was a Hebrew. And look, the right hand is huge. I wonder why?"

"Maybe there was a structural problem with the marble."

They slowly circled the statue viewing it from different angles, but soon, the room became crowded.

Delilah became agitated. "Too many people are squeezing into the museum. We must be on our way."

After walking back to the their hotel, they rested then waited for darkness and the dinner hour. Delilah felt her stomach rumbling. "I'm starving. I lust for the food in that lovely restaurant we found last night."

The following day, Jerry and Delilah placed their packs in a taxi, gave the driver instructions to the Villa Rossa hotel in Lucarelli and then they mounted their Treks and headed south. Fortunately, a bike path next to the sidewalk provided safe cycling, and before long, they rode beside the slow moving Arno river as it twisted its way through the city.

"I'm searching for a bridge near Bagno A Ripol," Delilah said. "Hopefully, we'll will see a sign."

A small span appeared on the right side of the road, and Jerry and Delilah joined the traffic moving upward. But another stream of cars funneled onto the bridge from a second ramp.

"This is dangerous," Delilah yelled. "Drivers entering the bridge from the right might not see us. Go slow! Go slow!"

"Is this the correct bridge?"

"I'm sure. I'm sure. Watch the cars. Go slow."

On reaching the other side of the Arno river, they felt relieved to see signs directing traffic southward toward Greve, the unofficial capital of the grape growing region in Chianti. They cycled onward, and after reaching the small town of Imprutneta, where early Christians hid in the brambles to escape from the Romans, they enjoyed pastry in a coffee shop, viewed the medieval Basilica Santa Maria dell Impruneta, then pedaled southward to Greve on the banks of a fast flowing river. Here, in the triangular shaped Piazza del Mercatolis, they locked their bikes in front of the quaint hotel Giovani de Verrazzno then climbed a staircase to a terraced restaurant with special views of the piazza and medieval buildings.

"Two tomato pastas and green salads," Deliah told the waiter. "I'm searching for the best tomato sauce in Tuscany."

"The best is here," the man replied. "My wife has cooking class. I bring taste. He disappeared but soon returned with a hot red liquid in a bowl, and promptly, Jerry and Delilah declared most delicious.

"You like?"

"Yes! Yes! Bring pasta."

Later, Delilah made her plea when the bill arrived. "I need the recipe for this wonderful pasta sauce."

"Wife show you. She has cooking class. Come. Come."

Delilah rose from the table and followed the waiter. "Leave a large tip then wait."

Soon, Delilah returned to the square grinning from ear to ear. "I have it. I'll make you the best tomato pasta in the world when we return home."

Jerry smiled. "I'm double-blessed. I have a beautiful woman who will cook wonderful pasta."

After cycling out of the piazza, Jerry and Delilah found themselves climbing again but soon rested at the famous winery Castella di Guerto and sampled extraordinary Chianti red wine.

"Don't drink too much," Deliah ordered. "We have a long day of cycling ahead."

Late in the afternoon, with the sun sinking toward the tuscan landscape, the Villa Rossa hotel appeared on the left side of the road. Ahead, the path ahead rose steeply into the hills. "That's the route to the walled city of Radda," Delilah said. "We're climbing there in the morning."

"Oh, God," Jerry muttered under his breath.

Jerry locked their bikes in the front courtyard while Delilah checked into the establishment. Beyond the desk, she noticed a lovely patio with tables prepared for dinners. "This is a beautiful hotel," she told the clerk.

Jerry and Delilah showered, rested, and later in the evening, as the moon rose high in the sky, they strolled into the patio for dinner bundled up with sweaters.

"We're in luck," Delilah whispered. "There is no menu."

Shortly, they began sipping delicious Chianti red wine, enjoyed green salads with a delicate olive oil, savored thick tuscan soup boiled down to a vegetable puree, relished thin slices of rare roast beef and consumed mounds of noodles mixed with a tangy pesto sauce. Apple tarts finished off the dinner.

Jerry squeezed Delilah arm. "I'm in heaven. We're eating our way through Tuscany. What are your plans for tomorrow?"

"We have an interesting and challenging day. First, we'll climb to Radda, and later in the morning, visit the walled town of Monteriggioni and enjoy lunch. Then, we'll face a long ride to San Gimignano, famous for its many medieval towers. It sits on a high plateau."

"Difficult climbing?"

"Yes, but I'm sure we can do it. We'll stay two nights at a beautiful place—the Hotel la Cisterna on the piazza.

The next morning, Jerry and Delilah climbed to Radda, rested and enjoyed the views of hills, villages and forests from high walls, loaded their seat packs with pastry then sped downhill to the small hamlet of Castellina in Chianti. Gratefully, they found themselves riding on flat terrain, gathered speed, and in late morning, reached Monteriggioni, a walled city rising high on a hill.

Pushing their bikes up a long steep road, they reached the piazza, walked to the precipice, viewed the scenery then found an outdoor restaurant for lunch.

Jerry sighed. "Let's try lasagne. I need a break from tomato pasta."

"I don't mind. I have my special recipe."

Rested, filled with body fuel for the rest of the day, Jerry and Delilah sped downhill then cycled for several hours on reasonably flat landscape filled with vineyards. The passed through the small town of Colle di Val d'Elsa, and then, in the afternoon, began a long unremitting climb toward San Gimignano. Its medieval towers rose higher and higher in the sky during their approach.

Jerry stopped and shouted. "I'm beat. I'm beat."

"OK. OK. Let's rest and eat and pastry. We need to gather

strength for the steep road ahead."

They leaned their bikes against a fence, sat on the ground, snacked, drank fluids, and in a little while, mounted their saddles and continued climbing. But now, they found themselves cycling in heavy traffic.

"There are too many cars," Delilah yelled. "Let's walk our bikes."

Moving toward the south gate of the city, they passed under a medieval archway then entered a narrow dark cobblestone street with ancient buildings rising on either side. A stream of tourists, finished for the day, descended on the left side of the path. On the right, walking almost alone, Jerry and Delilah struggled upward, bedraggled, exhausted and dripping with sweat.

People gaped at them, some offered the thumbs up sign while others approached their bikes applauding as if they rode the Tour de France. For those who cared to see, Jerry and Delilah were in the final stage of a magnificent ride to a fabled medieval town.

Jerry had a sly grin and turned to Delilah. "We've become a tourist attraction. These people are proud of us."

Delilah grabbed Jerry's neck, hugging him. "I'm proud of you too." Then, she poked her head into several stores to asking for directions. "Where is the Hotel la Cisterna?" Several clerks pointed their fingers straight ahead.

They pushed upward, moved under another archway cut into 13th century walls then entered a large piazza with many towers rising high above. They walked past a large well, found the hotel and pushed their bikes into the lobby where a bellboy grabbed their machines and placed them into storage.

Jerry and Delilah took their packs to a room on a high floor, showered, enjoyed the view of the piazza from a large window, then dressed for dinner. Soon, in an outdoor restaurant near the hotel, they seated themselves at a small table and waited for service. Jerry spoke in a weak voice. "I can barely move."

"You'll feel better with some food—order extra desserts."

Eating quietly, they watched tourists milling about the square. "We've had a tremendous experience climbing here," Jerry said while looking down at his plate. "But can't we skip tomorrow's ride and just explore this interesting town. There are many towers to examine."

Delilah nibbled at her food and seemed contemplative. "I don't think we should miss the gorgeous scenery in this area. These are beautiful hills all about."

"I can't call a taxi if my body collapse on a long climb."

"You'll feel better in the morning. Our exhaustion will disappear. We'll bring sandwiches and fruit. We're cycling south on a loop that returns here. We'll spend another night at the lovely hotel."

They both ate extra desserts then returned to their room. "Let's try getting 12 hours of sleep," Delilah advised. "Tomorrow's ride might prove difficult."

The next day, Jerry and Delilah pushed their bikes through the city's north gate, mounted saddles and began climbing a steep grade.

"This is a tough start, "Jerry shouted. "Is Tuscany one big hill?"

"I don't think so. Relax and pedal."

Eventually, the road level out, they cycled beside a green forest and soon reached a fork in the road. A sign read: Vicarello 20 kilometers. They noticed the route sweeping downhill. In awe, they stopped and gazed at the scenery. Below, as far as the eye could see, low hills, covered with greenery, extended outward and seemed to touch the pale blue sky.

"There they are," Delilah said in a quiet voice, "the green hills of Tuscany."

Jerry moved forward, grabbed Delilah's waist, and squeezed. "What a spectacular sight. They look like green sand dunes. Could they be green sand dunes?'

"Let's go. We're riding through the green hills of Tuscany."

Pointing their bikes downward, they gradually gathered speed.

Faster and faster, sweeping through the curves, power in their legs, Jerry and Delilah plunged into the colorful landscape and became thrilled with the descent. "Wow," Jerry screamed. "Wow. Wow!"

Soon, they arrived in the small hamlet of Vicarello and found an important road junction. A sign on the right pointed toward Voleterra and the route rose upward, curving out of sight.

"What type of town is Voleterra?" Jerry asked while nervously looking at the path to the right.

"It's a medieval city surrounded by ramparts and cliffs—a real tourist attraction. Let's see what it looks like."

They began a slow ascent, entered heavy traffic and switchbacks then decided to hug the edge of the road next to the mountain. About an hour later, they noticed ramparts and cliffs high above and Delilah stopped at a bar to ask for instructions.

"How far to Voleterra?" she asked a man, sitting at the bar. He gave them a queer look. "Three kilometers straight up."

"Voleterra is too far away and the road is too steep," Jerry blurted out . "Let's eat and return to the hotel. Its getting late. We can't cycle in the dark."

"OK! OK! You're right. We must reach the hotel in San Gimignano before twilight."

Jerry moved through a beaded curtain. "I smell wonderful food." He came back, grabbed Delilah's arm and pulled her to a table covered with a white cloth. "I'm hungry. Let's eat."

A waitress approached with a basket of bread, green olives in a bowl and a large menu. As usual, Delilah ordered for them both.

"Orange drinks, green salads and tomato pastas. Bring strawberry ice cream for dessert."

Soon, the waitress delivered drinks and salads, and a little later, presented one large bowl of steaming pasta. Chunks of fresh tomatoes floated in the sauce. Promptly, Delilah filled their plates using a large spoon and fork.

"This tastes delicious," Jerry exclaimed. "Is this the best tomato sauce in all of Tuscany?"

"It's good. But I like the tomato pasta in Greve a little better. It had more spice."

Jerry ordered extra ice cream to top off his blood sugar. "I'm worried," he said. "We have a long ride back to the hotel."

Soon, they cycled away from Voleterra downhill; and much of the afternoon, rode up and down steep hills. Then, near the end of the day, on a long descent, the towers of San Gimignano emerged below, ablaze in the sunset, like red torches reaching toward the sky.

Jerry pulled to the side of the road to rest. "Wow! Wow!" he screamed. Delilah squeezed his hand. "This is incredible. These medieval skyscrapers look like the city of Manhattan—on fire."

They cycled onward as the towers rose higher and higher, and then, in diminished light, passed under the north gate of San Gimignano, entered the piazza then collapsed in their room at the hotel.

"As usual," Jerry muttered, "the ride has drained every ounce of energy from our bodies. But what a great day. Not many people have seen the flaming towers of San Gimignano from seats of their bicycles."

They slowly peeled off their cycling outfits, showered, rested, dressed in slow motion, then drifted into the piazza searching for an outdoor restaurant. Jerry hung his head down. "You order for both of us. I'm too weak to make good choices."

"We need calories. I'll order beef and pasta. Let's pick double desserts."

They finished dinner then began a slow walk through the square with darkened towers rising high above. Delilah squeezed her body next to Jerry. "This is a spooky stroll."

"I agree. But what are your plans for tomorrow?"

"We're cycling to the beautiful city of Siena. The ride is short with flat or downhill terrain."

"That's good news."

"First, we'll reach the walled city of Monteriggioni, enjoy lunch, then ride on to experience market day in Siena. We should arrive at the hotel early in the afternoon."

In the morning, Delilah placed their packs in a taxi and instructed the driver to deliver them at the luxurious Jolly Hotel in the Piazza la Lizza.

They walked their bikes through the cobblestone street to the south gate, mounted saddles and sped downhill into cool morning air. After passing thorugh Colle di Vol d'Elsa and cycling for several hours, they found themselves looking up at huge promontory topped by Monteriggioni. Medieval walls surrounded the town.

They pushed their bikes up a steep road and entered a large piazza filled with souvenir shops and outdoor restaurants. Promptly, they peered over the precipice and enjoyed the view of the valley and sloping hills in the distance." I can't get enough of their this scenery," Jerry said.

"I'm starved. Let's eat."

Under a colorful awning whipped by the wind, Jerry and Delilah sat at table waiting for service. Jerry smiled. "I'm eating lasagne."

"OK. But let's order quickly, I want to shop in Siena's outdoor market."

"Will it stay open all day?"

"I don't know. Hopefully, we'll arrive early in the afternoon."

Jerry and Delilah finished lunch, sped downhill, entered flat terrain and picked up speed.

"'We're flying," Jerry yelled. "We're really flying."

Later, on a traffic circle in the outskirts of Siena, Delilah stopped in a gas station to ask for instructions. "Where is the Jolly hotel?" The attendant raised an arm and pointed it straight ahead. "Three kilometers."

Back in traffic, they found themselves squeezed to the curb by large trucks, but soon entered a bus-filled piazza, found the Hotel, then pushed their bikes into the lobby.

"You can't bring bicycles in here," the desk clerk screamed. "This is a four-star hotel."

A bellboy grabbed their bikes and rolled them into a storage room while Delilah collected keys to their rooms. Soon, they showered, pulled on walking shorts and headed for the outdoor market next to the square.

Music filled the air. Artists with accordions, violins, and other string instruments provided a joyous atmosphere. Vendor stalls, squeezed together, provided only a narrow passageway for buyers who anxiously examined good for sale. Delilah found a quilted white vest that she liked. "How much? Do you ship?" The vendor picked up the garment, turned it over and thought for awhile. "Thirty euros. I ship."

Jerry admired Delilah as she strutted in her new jacket. "You can wear that warm vest on cold winter mornings in Pittsburgh."

Moving slowly through the market, they examined many products especially pottery and art. But suddenly, extreme hunger forced them back into the piazza and into the medieval streets of Siena searching for a restaurant. "The food looks good here" Delilah said while examining tables in restaurant covered with a canopy.

Delilah ordered thick tuscan soup, tomato pasta and Jerry added grilled eggplant. But near the end of their meal, Delilah became pensive. "We should go back to the hotel and rest."

"Why. We've had only a short ride. Let's explore Siena."

"Tomorrow's ride is really long."

"How long?"

"At least 100 kilometers—maybe more."

"Tell me the bad news."

"We might be facing 70 or 80 miles of pedaling. I'm not really sure."

"Oh God. We can't climb that distance."

"It's not all hills. First, we'll cycle through small villages, head south, and hopefully, about noon, reach Pienza, a city built in the 15th century. It has commanding views of the valley from a high ridge. Next, we have a long ride and probably a steep climb to the small walled town of Monticehiello, and later, visit a larger walled city, Montepulciano. Then, we'll make a dash to our hotel, a luxurious, four-star villa just north of Chiusi, a railway hub. We'll enjoy a two night stay."

"What happens if I run out of gas?"

"Jerry, don't worry. We'll eat several lunches along the way. If you're in trouble, we'll stop at a bar and hire a van."

The next day, Jerry and Delilah cycled out of Siena in a dense fog, and nervously rode next to the curb until reaching the outskirts of the city.

"This is like biking through fogbound Pittsburgh," Delilah said. "It cool and dangerous—mainly dangerous."

After passing through small villages, they turned eastward, and late in the morning, stopped for sandwiches in the busy city of Asciano. While sitting on a bench in the square, Jerry struck up a conversation with tall twin cyclists from Holland. They had been touring Italy for one month, wore identical outfits and rode on yellow Canondale racing bikes.

"How does it feel to ride with one's mirror image," Jerry asked.

"Wonderful. I watch myself cycling all day and I'm never lonely."

Soon, they saddled up, and began long steep climb to Pienza, and on arrival, locked their bikes in a small park. Tour busses filled the small square.

After entering a cathedral and examining the tapestry, they walked on a path protected by a low stone wall and viewed the valley. Jerry leaned over the wall. "This is amazing. Did we really climb here?"

"Yes. Let's eat."

They enjoyed their traditional lunch, wandered among the old buildings and examined goods in shops but Delilah felt nervous. "We need to go. We are still facing a lot of cycling."

They plunged downhill, felt thrilled with the descent, and then, began climbing again on steep grades. At times, they dismounted and pushed their bikes, but eventually, approached Monticehiello, struggled up the road, but found the city almost deserted.

"This is a spooky place," Jerry said with some anxiety. "The climb here has been a waste of energy. Let's skip the next walled city. The day is almost gone."

"Jerry, please don't fret. I've been told that a great restaurant sits below the climb to Montepulciano. The food will give us energy for the end of the day."

"Oh, God. More climbing?"

"Yes. Let's' go. We must reach our hotel before twilight."

Continuing their journey, they cycled onward for another hour then noticed a restaurant surrounded by cars. A large terrace jutted out over the valley.

Jerry and Delilah locked their bikes, washed up in rest rooms, entered the establishment then found themselves greeted by wonderful odors from a food store holding with bins of breads, cheeses, olives, meats and fruits.

After passing through a large eating area filled with dinners, they stepped onto a terrace where most tables had magnificent views of the valley and the hills beyond. Delilah felt relieved. "What a wonderful setting for lunch. I'll order for us both. OK?"

"Sure. I'm too weak to think."

"Let's start with tomatoes topped with mozzarella cheese then sample their tomato pasta. OK."

"Sure. Let's eat?"

After savoring lunch, Jerry topped off his blood sugar with a large strawberry sundae. "Do you want one?"

"No. Eat and let's go. It's getting late in the day."

They cycled on a road that climbed continuously, and on arrival in Montepulciano, a tourist trap, Jerry rested on steps of a church while Delilah explored a few shops. She immediately returned. "Let's go. We must find the hotel as soon as possible. Drivers might not see us on the road after sunset."

They sped downhill, raced through the curves, and soon, reached the busy town of Chianciano Terme where Jerry rested and relieved his bladder in the bushes. Road signs, directing traffic toward Chiusi, seemed to calm their nerves.

"I'm not sure about the directions to the hotel," Delilah said. "I'll ask for instructions in that store across the street. She returned a few minutes later. "Saddle up. The clerk says the hotel is on the right side of the road across the street from a movie house."

They cycled onward and noticed the sun, an orange fireball, resting on the tuscan hills. A long thin line of reddish orange clouds gripped the horizon like a ragged red scarf.

Jerry, nearing exhaustion, pedaled slower and slower. Then, like a mime on wheels, he barely moved his legs, and then stopped. He placed both feet on the ground, straddled the top bar of his bike, cupped his hands around his mouth and yelled, "Delilah, I'm finished."

Turning around, Delilah rode back to Jerry, removed his helmet and wiped his face with a moist cloth. "Our hotel can't be more than one mile away. Rest, drink and take a bite of your energy bar."

Jerry placed his bike against a tree, sat on the curb and rested. "OK, I'll be ready to go in a few minutes. But please, don't race off and leave me in the dust."

Soon, they moved forward and noticed a movie theater on the left side of the road. On the right, sitting on a hill, a large red mansion rose toward the sky; and its gabled roof made it seem like castle in a Disney film. They had arrived—the Villa Il Patriaca.

Jerry and Delilah pushed their bikes up a long gravel driveway, parked them beside the front door, entered, and found a beautiful lobby with marble floors and glowing chandeliers. A bellboy grabbed their bikes for storage as Delilah approached the desk with passports. She turned toward Jerry. "I'm glad to see our packs in the hall."

A maid led them to their room on the top floor, and here, Delilah found antique furniture, a high ceiling and a large window that opened outward. She released a shutter that exposed a large garden filled with flowering plants, green bushes, benches and walking paths. Beyond, the hills of Tuscany, bathed in long black shadows, sat under a twilight sky, a Monet sky, that blessed the earth with colors of lavenders and pinks.

In the bathroom, Delilah found a wide nozzle that extended downward from the ceiling toward a huge square tub. She smiled. "This shower is big enough for two."

"You go first. My body is limp—totally limp."

Dressed for dinner, they strolled into the garden, walked on a path to watch the afterglow, then sat on a bench and reminisced about their extraordinary day.

Jerry spoke with a low weak voice. "I feel proud to have survived 10 hours of cycling. "I'm happy that this hotel provides a two night stay. I certainly need a day of rest."

"Jerry, you have good reason to feel proud. In the morning, we'll soak up sunshine in this beautiful garden, rest and walk. But I have a surprise for you."

"A surprise?"

"Yes. The day after tomorrow, we'll cycle for a few miles to Chiusi with packs on our backs then ride a train to the lake district in Northern Italy for gentle biking beside blue waters."

"How long?"

"I don't know. Let's see how we feel."

"And then?"

"We might store our bikes in a hotel then take a train to Chamonix to hike in the Alps."

"That sounds terrific. We'll enjoy an endless summer. Right?"

"Maybe. But added days in Europe might delay your search for a publisher and a teaching position in a medical school."

"No problem. I have an excellent literary agent who is circulating my work. Also, I can apply to a university later in the fall since physical diagnosis is taught in spring. I'll have the necessary resourses to provide for you."

"Am I hearing a marriage proposal?"

"Yes. I need to hold you at night—every night. I must see your lovely face in the morning—each morning. If you like, we'll make all the wedding arrangements on arrival back in Pittsburgh."

"Jerry, you are a loving, eloquent and romantic man. Yes, I intend to be your wife."

Unnoticed, darkness slowly slipped into the garden, and Jerry rose from the bench with swirling thoughts of a happy life. Bending over, he kissed Delilah lightly on the lips, gently lifted her, and then, arm in arm, shuffled down the blackend path toward the glittering lights at the hotel.

Soon, at a corner table in the dining room, Jerry and Delilah began sipping champagne and discussing their impending marriage. Clicking glasses, they toasted to their new adventures: "To our endless summer."

Chapter Thirteen

THE FALLING

Delilah dressed early in the morning then patiently waited for Jerry to wake up. Finally, she shook his shoulder. "Jerry, get up. Let's eat breakfast and walk in the garden."

Jerry stirred then rose to the side of the bed. "I have a bad headache. I don't feel well."

"You can rest all day. Tomorrow, you'll feel better. Get up and dress. I'm hungry."

"What's your name? I just can't remember."

"Delilah. My name is Delilah. I hope you're not you're not losing your memory again."

"I'm not sure. I have a bad headache."

"Jerry, say something for me."

"What?"

"Around the rugged rock the rapid rabbit ran."

"Around—around."

"Oh my God! Jerry, something must have plugged the shunt in your brain. Your ventricle must be expanding again."

"My what?"

"Doctor McGinness placed a shunt into the ventricle of your brain to relieve pressure caused by hydrocephalus. Remember?"

"No. I don't remember."

"Look, Delilah said, "this is serious. I'm taking our bikes to a cycling shop in Chiusi for shipment to Pittsburgh. Then, we're riding a train to Florence and flying to Dulles International Airport as soon as possible. Get dressed. I'll be back after delivering our bikes. Please pack and be ready to catch the train."

Delilah obtained the address of a cycling shop from the clerk at the desk, hired a taxi, then delivered the bikes for shipment to the United States. Promptly, she returned to the hotel, packed, and with Jerry in tow, rode a taxi to the train station in Chiusi.

"You have a shunt in your brain that needs to be flushed out," she told Jerry. "It's a simple procedure. You'll be fine. I'll take you to the hospital when we arrive in Pittsburgh."

Jerry and Delilah took the first train to Florence, slept overnight in a hotel, and in the morning, flew to Washington D.C. on an Austrian Airline jet. They retrieved their van then drove to Pittsburgh where Delilah deposited Jerry in the emergency room. Here, a physician examined Jerry and immediately called Doctor McGinness who arranged for the hospitalization; and that night, Delilah slept on a cot beside Jerry's bed.

In the morning, Doctor McGinness examined Jerry."I'm going to order an MRI scan of your brain and return later in the day. Also, I'm asking your neurologist to see you again."

In the afternoon, Doctor McGinness returned to Jerry's room and presented his report: "Your hydrocephalus has become worse! Also, there is blood floating inside the ventricle. Probably, a clot of blood has blocked the opening in the shunt. I'll flush it out in the morning. Surgery is scheduled for eight a.m."

Delilah frowned. "Why is he bleeding?"

"Small blood vessels in the wall of the ventricle are probably fragile," Doctor McGinness replied. "They might have been damaged by trauma during his auto accident several years ago. Irrigation of the shunt should establish good drainage of ventricular fluid into the abdomen and allow his memory to return. Delilah, I'll see you in the family surgical lounge about nine a.m."

Doctor McGinnes turned, left the room, and in the little while, the neurologist arrived to examine Jerry. "Doctor Stern, are you having trouble walking again?"

"I'm stumbling."

"I see. Please walk a bit for me. That's good. Yes. Your gait has become weird again. Now, say for me the following statement: Around the rugged rock the rapid rabbit ran."

"Around—around."

"That's OK. Doctor McGinness should correct this problem when he irrigates the shunt in the morning. Your ventricles will shrink and your memory will return."

The next day, Delilah waited in the surgical lounge with increasing anxiety, and after a considerable length of time, Doctor McGinness arrived. He approached Delilah while looking at the ground. "The shunt remains blocked. I'm sure it's plugged with clotted blood. I couldn't insert a new shunt because the procedure would cause dangerous bleeding. Also, it would become blocked again."

"What are you going to do next?" Delilah asked in a pleading voice. "Jerry must regain his memory."

"I'm sorry. I don't have an answer at this time. I did everything possible to open the shunt with high pressure irrigations. It has remained plugged. Also, I spoke with one of my colleagues at the Mayo clinic and offered to transfer Jerry to that facility if he had an alternate surgical procedure. He didn't have any suggestions. He agreed that blood would block any new shunt placed into the ventricle. Furthermore, I have asked two other neurosurgeons to render separate opinions regarding Jerry's condition. They will examine him, review his brain scans and evaluate his chart. I've refrained from placing a negative prognosis on paper so that they might give unbiased opinions. In addition, I'll discuss Jerry's problem with his neurologist, Doctor Smith. I'm very sorry. I have nothing to offer at this time."

"Nothing to offer?"

"I'm sorry. Let's wait to hear from the other neurosurgeons. They might have some helpful ideas."

Doctor McGinness turned to leave the room. "I'll see Jerry in the morning."

Stunned, Delilah sat in the chair and stared out at the green courtyard through an open window. "How is it possible for a man to rise out of the abyss, recover, enjoy life, become a lover, an athlete, and then plunge back into darkness?", she asked herself. "Now, he's back in the void. It's not fair. It's not fair."

Delilah wept uncontrollably. "It's not fair. It's not fair."

Soon, she composed herself then returned to Jerry's room to await visits by the other neurosurgeons. Eventually, they examined Jerry and indicated their opinions would be placed on the chart. They both told Delilah that alternate procedures were not available to treat Jerry's condition.

The next day, Jerry had another MRI scan of the brain and Doctor Terrance Smith returned to evaluate him again.

"Doctor Stern's ventricles are continuing to expand," he said. "Delilah, may I speak with you in the hall."

Dutifuly, Delilah followed Doctor Smith who put his arm around her shoulder. "The increasing pressure in the ventricles might cause coma and sudden death."

"Jerry is going to die?" Delilah asked almost shouting.

"The enlarging ventricles might force brain tissue downwards to the base of the skull and compress the breathing center in the midbrain. This event is named, 'herniation through the tentorium!' It is possible, however, that the chambers might stabilize. I think we've done everything possible to help Jerry. He'll need care in a nursing home."

"Return to Heavenly Manor?"

"Under the circumstances, I don't believe you will be able to care for him at home. He likely has a terminal illness."

Delilah returned to the room and found Jerry in bed with his face buried in a pillow. Jerry said, "I have a headache and need to sleep."

Delilah looked at the floor. "I'm going home. I'll see you in the morning."

Drained, Delilah threw herself on a bed and wept on and off. She slept for awhile but the telephone jolted her into an upright position.

"This is Leon," the voice said over the line. "How are you, Delilah?"

"Not good, Leon. Doctor Smith thinks Jerry needs terminal care at Heavenly Manor. The surgeon can't drain his ventricles because of blood in the chamber."

Leon answered in a low voice, almost inaudible. "That's awful news. I'm calling because Simon and Shuster has agreed to publish Jerry's book. They need to know if he will tour with the work. What shall I tell them?"

"I would say that Jerry is ill at the present time. If he is unable to travel, I'll promote the book. Tell them that I'm his nurse and know every word in the manuscript. I'll do it. I'll make Jerry famous and complete his mission in life."

"OK, I'll call them back and present your response. Also, I'll write a formal letter that will obligate you to tour with the book."

"That's fine, Leon. I'll advance Jerry's cause through the length and breadth of this nation. I'll help Jerry turn back the medical clock to the 19th century when physicians diagnosed at the bedside. Believe me, I'll get his message out."

"Delilah, that's great. But I need to tell you something else. Jerry left a will and you are his sole heir of all his property including the book. Essentially, you will be touring with your own property."

"My God. What irony."

"When will the book appear in print?"

"About 90 days."

"OK, Leon, I've retired as a nurse. Now, I'll dedicate myself to bring physicians back to the bedside. Jerry will live on in another way."

The telephone rang again and Delilah picked up the receiver with trepidation, and heard the voice of Terrance Smith.

"Is anything new?" she asked.

"No. I've spoken with Doctor McGinness and he doesn't have anything else to offer and neither do the consulting neurosurgeons. I would like to transfer Jerry to Heavenly Manor in the morning. Is that all right?"

"What time?"

"Nine a.m."

"OK. I'll be there. I need to speak with Jerry before he leaves."

Early the next day, an attendant pushed a wheelchair into Jerry's room.

"He's taking you back to Heavenly Manor," Delilah said in a trembling voice.

"Heavenly Manor? Heavenly Manor?"

"Yes, Jerry. They will care for you until you feel better. I have good news. Simon and Shuster will publish your book."

"My book? My book?"

"Yes, *The Romance of Bedside Diagnosis* will be published soon."

The attendant spoke firmly. "Please, we must leave."

Jerry rose from the bed, sat in the chair, and promptly, the man wheeled him around then disappeared through the door as Delilah placed her head in her hands and wept for a long, long time.

Chapter Fourteen

THE FOG

Several weeks later, Doctor Smith called Delilah at home in the evening.

"Doctor Thompson, the director of Heavenly Manor, spoke with me today," he said. "I have been informed that Jerry is sleeping a great deal during the day, and this change in his condition might signal impending coma. I thought it best to relay this message to you."

Delilah remained silent for several seconds before speaking. "I greatly appreciate your call. I need to see Jerry one more time and will drive to Heavenly Manor in the morning. I want to take this opportunity to express to you my gratitude for all the medical help you have offered."

Early after dawn, Delilah dressed in a freshly starched white uniform, pulled on a heavy coat then stepped outside into dense swirling fog. She could barely see her van sitting in the driveway. She started the engine, warmed it up, then slowly drove into the street to join bumper to bumper traffic that slowly moved in the gloom.

"Today," Delilah said to herself, "the rivers have released a terrible fog that adds to my burdens. Now, I making my last visit to Heavenly Manor in dangerous conditions. I loved Jerry from the moment he touched my face. For sure, I knew, a demented man would never make a pass at me. And what a thrill it was to watch him emerge from Alzheimer's disease after Doctor Smith drained his spinal fluid. Yes, Jerry desperately loved me and I desperately loved him back. I loved him even more after that hard training ride to the trout farm where he cried over his fish as the water wheel sprayed us with mist. He looked so cute.

In the Czech Republic, on that difficult 50 mile ride into Prague, it seemed like a miracle that he survived considering his weakened physical condition, and that evening, in the lounge of the hotel, I loved the way he held me on the dance floor. And later in the week, at the Czech border, Jerry became ecstatic when we plunged into Austria with those spectacular vineyards rising up to meet us. He screamed, 'Yahoo! Yahoo!

And that night in Vienna, that special evening at the Blue Duck Restaurant, I held him tightly and wrapped my arms around his neck while dancing to Edith Piaf's song, 'La vie en Rose.' I said, 'Jerry, I'll never let you go.'

But Jerry, I now must let you go. I need to let you go. I can't bear watching you slide away.

Jerry loved France, especially the small village of St. Saturnin les Apt—the restaurants, the climb to the ruins of the castle and the ride to the Col du Murs. He relished visiting the red village of Roussillon and the artist colony at Joucas. For me, Joucas seemed mystical and special.

In St. Remy's outdoor market, Jerry acted like a kid shopping in a candy store, tasting food right and left. He liked the poet too. Later, we climbed to that high ridge in Les Baux, and he felt wonderful among the pink ruins of the Roman fortress with the wind blowing in his face.

We didn't stay long in that old farm house in the vineyards, but Jerry savored making love in that four-poster bed. And when he pulled me into that double shower, he held me so tightly that my body almost soared to heaven on a plume of hot steam.

What a spectacular ride we had to Nimes, and on the return, Jerry blocked the wind for me while climbing away from the city. For sure, he had became a great athlete and a great cyclist. And at the wine cooperative, nearing collapse, I loved the way he ate nougat bars. He didn't just nibble, he demolished then with huge bites to gather strength for the final ride home.

Tuscany seemed like a mixed bag—good and bad. Jerry loved the food but hated walking among the mobs of tourists. He felt estatic among the green hills and on on that long ride around San Gimignano, he saw the towers ablaze at sunset.

But alas, our visit to Tuscany ended in tragedy when blood blocked his shunt. One day I had a lover and a great athlete as a companion, and the next morning, traveled with a severely compromised man who required hospitalization. What a shock. We had so much living and loving left in our lives. And now, despite the best surgical efforts, Jerry has been slipping away. All that remains is his book, *The Romance of Bedside Diagnosis.* I swear by all that is sacred, by God in heaven, that I'll make this piece of Jerry last a long time. But now, this morning, on this terribly foggy morning, I'll hold my my Jerry, my love, one last time."

The fog slowly lifted, Delilah sped forward, and soon, Heavenly Manor appeared on a hill, rising above the mist. She parked the van, entered the building, hung her coat on a rack then walked up the steep staircase to the high floor housing patients with Alzheimer's disease. She reached the dark oak door, rang a bell and patiently waited for admission. Promptly, she approached an elderly nurse sitting at a desk.

"I'm Delilah," she said. "I'm here to see Doctor Jerome Stern."

"I've heard of you. You're the one who snatched him away from Heavenly Manor. He belongs here, you know."

"Yes, I understand that his condition has deteriorated. I need to see him one last time. May I give him medications this morning?"

"He's been taken off of all drugs since he sleeps most of the day."

"Let me have some juice."

The nurse opened a small refrigerator, poured liquid into a cup, placed it on a tray, then handed it to Delilah who quickly turned and walked down the hall.

Delilah knocked on the door of room 14, pushed open the door and found Jerry in bed, dozing.

Delilah smiled. "I'm a temporary nurse. I've brought you some refreshments."

"Where's the fat one?"

"She's off for awhile and will be back later in the day. Here, drink this juice. It's good for you."

"What your name? You're so beautiful."

"My name is Delilah."

Jerry sat bolt upright, drained the cup. "What's your name? You're so beautiful.?"

"My name is Delilah."

"May I touch your face? You're so beautiful."

"Yes, you may touch my face."

Jerry lifted a shaking hand toward Delilah and gently caressed her cheek with his finger tips. "You're so beautiful."

"What's your name?," Delilah asked.

"Jerry. My name is Jerry."

"Jerry, may I touch your face?"

"Sure. Sure."

Deliah lifted her hand and stroked Jerry's chin, lips and nose. "May I hug you?"

"Sure. Sure."

Delilah grabbed Jerry, crushed him to her body, held his head with one hand, then bent over his shoulders convulsively weeping.

"Delilah, it's all right. It's all right."

She released him. "I must go. I'm just a temporary nurse filling in on this shift."

Delilah quickly turned, didn't look back, opened the door, hurried through the corridor, then sped down the staircase vowing never to return to Heavenly Manor.

EPILOGUE

A tall white-haired man, dressed in a dark blue suit, strode to the rostrum and banged the gavel down.

"I now call to order the 103rd meeting of the Alleghaney medical society. Tonight, we have gathered here to honor the life and work of Doctor Jerome Stern, esteemed specialist in internal medicine and infectious diseases. Recently, Simon and Schuster published his book, *The Romance of Bedside Diagnosis*. His nurse, Delilah, will discuss Doctor Stern's career and mention his inspiring volume, which you will have an opportunity to buy after our business meeting. But before she comes to the podium, I would like everyone to stand to pay homage to our colleague with a moment of silence."

Men and women stood up, bowed their heads, and then, after several minutes, returned to their seats.

"Now," the chairman said, "I am privileged to ask Delilah to come forward."

"I am grateful for the opportunity to speak with you tonight," Delilah said to the audience. "Doctor Jerome Stern began his career in academic medicine, and 10 years later, after losing research grants, bought a small black bag, filled it with diagnostic instruments, then opened an office to practice internal medicine and infectious diseases. One his last day of academic's life, he felt despair, since for a long time, he had dreamt of becoming a full professor of medicine. But as he finished his packing, a friend called and begged him to visit his wife who had been hospitalized in the suburbs suffering with fever, chest pains, and shortness of breath. She had been diagnosed as a case of double pneumonia.

Doctor Stern arrived at the hospital, performed a secret consultation, and at the bedside, diagnosed myocarditis, pericarditis, heart failure and pulmonary edema. After considerable persuasion, the patient agreed to transfer to the university hospital for emergency treatment. Then, he drove to the airport to begin a new life. He felt that academic medicine had been prologue, just prologue.

Yes, Doctor Stern's career at the university had been prologue for he soon developed a gratifying private practice, and interestingly enough, continued scholarly pursuits. Over the years, he published 11 scientific articles, presented 13 papers at national medical meetings and even discovered a new method of using the stethoscope.

As you know, Rene Laennec, invented the stethoscope in 1819 and described ausculatation of the lungs. He advised physicians to examine the chest with patients placed upright. But Doctor Stern found that by performing auscultations of the lungs in the lateral decubitus positions (the side positions), the hidden crackling sounds of early pneumonia could be heard.

It seems amazing, but true, that even after a passage of 186 years since the invention of the stethoscope, and examinations of patients by millions of physicians, no one else had observed the value of Doctor Stern's method of searching for early pneumonia."

Doctor Stern firmly believed in the magic of the physical examination and held as his hero Sir William Osler who helped establish the American system of medical education at the end of the 19th century. But in the middle of a productive medical practice, Jerome Stern suffered a loss of memory, a hospital canceled his privileges, the state lifted his medical license and the court placed him in a nursing home diagnosed as a case of Alzheimer's disease.

Fortunately, a brilliant neurologist correctly diagnosed normal pressure hydrocephalus. Soon, with the placement of a drainage shunt into the ventricle of his brain, Doctor Stern regained his memory, dictated his book, then traveled to Europe on a cycling journey with a new love. He biked between Prague and Vienna, cycled among the beautiful perched villages in Southern France then challenged the green hills of Tuscany.

In Italy, however, tragedy struck Doctor Stern when blood blocked his shunt, causing loss of memory. Then, despite the best neurosurgical efforts, his ventricles expanded and eventually induced coma and death. Yes, he prematurely lost his life but the message lives on in his book,

The Romance of Bedside Diagnosis. I would like to read for you the epilogue of this uplifting work."

I remember the emotions when the university snatched its position from beneath my feet. With a professorship beyond my grasp, I hung a shingle, carried a black bag and focused creative energies on physical examination—the essence of the art of medicine.

Over the years, I've had many dark hours while searching for diagnoses but William Osler's legacy of bedside sleuthing guided me like a divine light. And since my early teachers had links with this professors' protégés at John Hopkins Hospital, I've felt proud to be part of this heritage.

Intuitively, patients appreciate the merits of the physical examination and trust grows as physicians probe with care. A long time ago, a discouraged patient entered my office with six months of low-grade fever.

"Those red lumps on your legs are called erythema nodosum, signs of histopasmosis, a deep fungal infection," I told the patient.

Suddenly, she sobbed uncontrollably on the table and said that no other doctor had performed a thorough physical examination.

During the battle against disease, attachments may develop between the healer and the sick, and often, feelings of affection may emerge. Occasionally, while pushing patients along paths toward recovery, I've said, "I love you," and once, to block an unnecessary amputation of a leg, a patient heard from my lips that she was the most beautiful girl on the earth. These remarks begged for trust. Thus, physicians and patients, bonded together, sail on a voyage that flees the Grim Reaper.

Curiously enough, I presented two papers at the same medical meeting in my 14th year of private practice, and as time passed, my office swirled with manuscripts that became the basis for many scientific articles and numerous presentations at national medical meetings. My internist's life and a professorship without portfolio became exciting, and frequently, I mailed an enlarging curriculum vitae to universities searching for another post. But like bottled messages thrown into ragging seas, these letters evoked no response.

But rapidly, I became disabled, and with no other choice, closed my office but felt proud to have practiced a cherished and most enduring art. While thoughts of great cases have soothed my troubled soul, I suffered pain, almost like an amputation, after packing away my medical bag.

For years, this small case had been part of my body, and then suddenly, it disappeared and left a terrible open wound. Perhaps, I thought, proud flesh might eventually fill the void. Yes, I had loved my black bag—dearly loved it after all.

But now, I've entered the third millennium without my patients, but my spirit lingers, still lingers in the world of 19th century medicine where physicians enjoyed the romance of bedside diagnosis and harkened to William Osler's plea for his profession: 'To serve the art of medicine as it should be served, one must love his fellow-men."

Indeed, Doctor Jerome Stern served the art of medicine with distinction, and he truly loved his fellow-men. He left us a gift, his book—*The Romance of Bedside Diagnosis*."

Delilah took her seat as the audience rose with a standing ovation. And later, she sold many books then left the hall with a renewed spirit. "My Jerry lives on," she told herself. "My Jerry lives on."

ALSO BY VERNE E. GILBERT, M.D.
Senior Sporting Adventures